NOBODY LOOKS THAT YOUNG HERE

ESSENTIAL PROSE SERIES 147

 Canada Council Conseil des Arts
for the Arts du Canada

 ONTARIO ARTS COUNCIL
CONSEIL DES ARTS DE L'ONTARIO
an Ontario government agency
un organisme du gouvernement de l'Ontario

Canadä

Guernica Editions Inc. acknowledges the support of the Canada Council for the Arts and the Ontario Arts Council. The Ontario Arts Council is an agency of the Government of Ontario.

We acknowledge the financial support of the Government of Canada.

NOBODY LOOKS THAT YOUNG HERE

DANIEL PERRY

GUERNICA EDITIONS
TORONTO · BUFFALO · LANCASTER (U.K.)
2018

Copyright © 2018, Daniel Perry and Guernica Editions Inc.
All rights reserved. The use of any part of this publication,
reproduced, transmitted in any form or by any means, electronic,
mechanical, photocopying, recording or otherwise stored
in a retrieval system, without the prior consent
of the publisher is an infringement of the copyright law.

This is a work of fiction. Names, characters, places and incidents either
are the product of the author's imagination or are used fictitiously.

Michael Mirolla, editor
David Moratto, interior and cover design
Guernica Editions Inc.
1569 Heritage Way, Oakville, (ON), Canada L6M 2Z7
2250 Military Road, Tonawanda, N.Y. 14150-6000 U.S.A.
www.guernicaeditions.com

Distributors:
University of Toronto Press Distribution,
5201 Dufferin Street, Toronto (ON), Canada M3H 5T8
Gazelle Book Services, White Cross Mills
High Town, Lancaster LA1 4XS U.K.

First edition.
Printed in Canada.

Legal Deposit – First Quarter
Library of Congress Catalog Card Number: 2017960392
Library and Archives Canada Cataloguing in Publication
Perry, Daniel, 1982-
[Short stories. Selections]
Nobody looks that young here / Daniel Perry.

(Essential prose series ; 147)
Short stories.
Issued in print and electronic formats.
ISBN 978-1-77183-251-9 (softcover).--ISBN 978-1-77183-252-6 (EPUB).
-- ISBN 978-1-77183-253-3 (Kindle)

I. Title. II. Series: Essential prose series ; 147

PS8631.E77933A6 2018   C813'.6   C2017-907295-1   C2017-907296-X

For my parents, with love

*L'adolescence ne laisse un bon souvenir
qu'aux adultes ayant mauvaise mémoire.*
—**François Truffaut**

Contents

Projections	1
Territory	13
Five Stages of Sorry	25
Respect	43
Big Man	45
Bondo	53
Tabaco Babies	65
Eyesore	75
Hyperbolic	83
Mercy	97
Young Buck	123
Swept Up	141
The Expiry Dates	149
Precision	161
Comets	169
Ode	179
Nobody Looks That Young Here	195
Afterword	207
About the Author	211

Projections

YOU'VE ALWAYS PRESUMED there's a Highway 402, but as it's nowhere near Toronto you were never sure. No loss. It's not a lifeline like 401 or even 403 — it's just four empty lanes over a hundred flat kilometres, London to the border at Sarnia. It closes off a triangle on the map with its thick blue strip and Old 40, Sarnia to Chatham, and the 401 from Chatham to London, a shape with no more lines inside it. The old roads are still there, but now maintenance is up to the counties. The counties have let the asphalt crumble.

Currie — *Your Town*, you call it — is dead centre of the triangle, Exit 60 off 402. The sign still reads *Population 20,000*, but these days I doubt it's five. In the windows of the yellow brick movie theatre, bed sheets sag and reveal the lobby floor littered with cheap toys that belong to the new owner's kids. Behind the black double doors at the back, the forty red seats sit as empty as they did when they were mine.

IN CURRIE, IF you don't work at the Ritter Pulley plant or teach school you're likely unemployed. You might commute one way or the other on 402, or you might have retired here for the quaint small-town life you now know is a myth. This place is nothing like Muskoka or where you skied in Vermont: no beaches, no mountains, and an hour's drive from one not-so-Great Lake or the other. There isn't even a weathered copy of the *Currie Township Seed-Tribune* to flutter down the empty street, template headline THANK YOU [BUSINESS NAME] FOR [NUMBER OF YEARS], because last year, 2008, the *Seed-Tribune* was that business.

Teenagers are all that drifts through town now. They work briefly at Canada's smallest Canadian Tire or the Giant Tiger store, the Tim Hortons or McDonalds rest stops on the highway, and either blow all their money on movies at the Forest City Eightplex in London or save it to get the hell out of here.

MY OLDER BROTHER Scott had it figured, I think. He was nearly eighteen when he bought the rusty VW bus from Herm Mueller's scrapyard and agreed to pay in labour. I was fourteen then, and stupid, so I believed him when he told me that if I covered his shifts the days he couldn't work I'd get to drive it too, once I had my licence. We spent months fixing it up, and the day it finally turned over was pretty much the last I saw of Scott. He left one night and didn't call until three days later, from the roadside in Tennessee with Claire Burford, who I'd call his girlfriend except that officially, as a cop's kid, she was off-limits. They were trying to get to California but had mistaken the route. Scott said, "It was all Claire's idea," and not much else—that I should tell Mom and Dad he was okay, but not where he was.

THREE YEARS PASSED before we heard from him again. I'd stayed on at Mueller's to pay off Scott's van, and had also come into a grumbly Thunderbird that drank gas like a rubby. For a while Claire's old man stopped by daily, asking when *that asshole brother* of mine was bringing her home, but otherwise I just tinkered every day, pulling pieces off wrecks and dropping cash into the toolbox Herm paid me from. My share went through my carburetor and the Eightplex wicket, which were stupid ways to use it as Ryerson had accepted my what-the-heck application to their brand-new economics program. It was late summer and I was packing when Scott called from Calgary, where he had settled.

"Toronto?" he said. "That's where Claire is—in The Beaches. She married that doctor and had kids. You should look her up."

In my mind, like everyone from Currie still does, Claire looked exactly as she did the day she finished high school—never mind what might have happened since she'd run off on Scott in New Mexico with some med student in a convertible, I imagined her standing near water and gazing into the din of the city. Her orange sundress billowed in the lake breeze. Her long chestnut hair ruffled.

"You still talk?" I said.

"Yeah, sometimes. We send emails."

"You're not mad at her?"

"Are you kidding? She got me out of Currie Township."

In the background I heard a woman's voice, but not what she was saying.

"Got to go, Dave. When do you leave again?"

"Tomorrow morning."

"Don't ever go back," he said.

When the call disconnected I felt like Duane from *Last Picture Show*. Leaving Currie for Toronto and a degree didn't seem so different than leaving Anarene for the war, but I didn't say I was staying away forever; it was open-ended, like all the best goodbye scenes. I did make myself one promise, though: if I returned, I would never lord my education over people. Currie already had one Phil Purvis, at the bank, and he was good at drowning family farms and closing small shops by rejecting loan applications.

Had I really intended to come home, I'd have studied history or English — something I could teach. But after what happened with Jeanie Winter, I was pretty sure I wouldn't be back.

THE WIZARD CINEMA in Currie shut down for the first time just after Scott left, when I had been old enough to go to movies alone for two years. It changed the meaning of *old enough* to *driver's licence* overnight. I filled the next two summers with baseball and a winter and a half with hockey before replacing them with drinking and smoking, as everyone did eventually. To do anything — go bowling, see a band, eat something other than pizza or Wang's Chinese — the first step was to get away from this town and the fading *For Sale* sign in the theatre window. But as it was 1976, I was stuck in ninth grade science class with a sickening crush on the studious blonde at the desk in front of mine. We capped the school year with a kiss in the gym as we slow-danced to "Free Bird".

You're laughing, but that's all right. Jeanie would be, too. My parents put no stock in the relationship and neither did hers; we'd have probably wound up married, but we were just kids. Who's to say how it would've gone? I have a picture in a shoebox somewhere, but I don't look at it every night and miss her, no matter the sentimental bullshit you'll hear in Currie Township — and for someone gone as long as I've been, enough crops up.

It's like this: her death was my fault. I spent a few months afterward wandering room to room in my parents' house — not grieving anymore, just feeling guilty — and I honour her memory with a donation to the charity the obituary suggests every time the *London Free Press* website runs the familiar headline: *Currie teen killed in crash.*

It's always late summer, always around twilight, rock radio spilling out open windows and more kids than seatbelts in the car. In a dark grove of pines just before London, your highway swallows ours on a small hill and traffic bottlenecks. Everyone wants off 402. And once a year, a teenager fresh from the road test ploughs into the last car in line. I sign my donation, *With sympathy and understanding, Dave McLaren*, because in 1978, I was the one driving. I braked fast enough to minimize the impact and in the backseat, Claire's sister Susan, Ray Tarkington and Hank Mueller were fine. So was I, and so was Garth Callaghan, who was belted shotgun. Jeanie, by then my girlfriend of two years, was unsecured on his lap. She died instantly when she was launched through the windshield, out of Currie Township head first.

IT TURNED OUT that, after its first closure, the Wizard hadn't sat empty all those years: the owner, Abe Clark, had been living inside. He was the same age as my grandparents, who remembered his opening after the War in the forties and the cars streaming in from the township, the farm families in Sunday best. Abe was all smiles then, my Grandma Mary told me, and she and Grandpa Marvin would take Mom and her brothers every Saturday. Mom says, though, that by the time she was going alone, Abe had put his still-original staff out front to tear tickets while he hid at the concession booth and gruffly filled popcorn bags.

Mom says it didn't matter what was playing, or what was new—only that there were movies. I'm sure I didn't mind *Bambi* replays when I was little, and later, I saw *2001* way too many times in a Wizard empty save for me and Garth and of course, old Abe. His face was wizened and angular by then, and he had lost all his hair except for the long white ring behind his ears that frayed as he sniffed and grunted, now back to taking tickets. *Taxi Driver* was the last movie I saw there, and popcorn was on the honour system: self-serve, put a dollar in the jar. It didn't start on time because Abe was the only person working there and we had to wait for him to lock the booth and lumber up the stairs to the projector room.

THE FALL AFTER my accident, Currie High School's Welcome Back Assembly was a safe driving presentation as it has been every year since. That November I bought a used Chevette and took a job delivering pizzas. People picked up their orders themselves in town, so I did all my driving in the country with steaming boxes stacked on the front seat as I searched dark gravel roads for houses hundreds of yards back, pale in their barn lights. I preferred scouring the countryside to the lonely trips back to town, though, where every time I glanced sideways I'd see only the empty seat.

With this job, I saved, and when I had enough for the summer's rent in Toronto I sold the car and bought a train ticket. People might have talked less the longer I stayed, but only because there'd have been no one left who hadn't heard I was the guy who killed poor Jeanie Winter. In time, every secret gets dug up from Currie Township's black clay.

AFTER GRADUATING I took the first offer I got, crunching numbers for TD in a tower on Bay Street. I'd worked there three months when my mother's call came. Abe's body had been found in the theatre. Apparently, some kids had heard the projector was still inside and they broke in one Friday night to steal it. The story goes that when they opened the doors the smell made them throw up. No one knows how long he'd been dead.

With my shiny new degree, Mom thought I'd be perfect to resurrect the Wizard. Post-secondary might be expected in Toronto, but it's an oddity where I come from, so Purvis would lend money to anyone who had graduated — no matter the major. On top of this, Mom had already talked to him, and the *Seed-Tribune*'s only reporter, too. They all seemed to agree that a movie theatre would keep the kids off the streets, which to them wasn't just an expression — Mom claimed eleven-to-sixteen-year-olds were roaming Main Street in packs, and sometimes spending whole afternoons just sitting on a curb. Someone had to do something, she said. I said I'd think about it — even then, businesses didn't open in Currie, they closed one-by-one. The last new independent was Magnum Video; the pizza joint had changed names and owners so often it called *itself* The Pizza Joint. There were otherwise just five occupied storefronts: Wang's, Brewskie's Bar, Price-Mart Grocery, Darla's Flowers and the coffee shop where the farmers still eat in dwindling numbers on weekends, Don's Breakfast. A walk down Main Street meant remembering old signs above the rest of the store windows, all papered-over, and dresses or sporting goods or musical instruments inside.

Main Street wasn't the road I was worried about, though.

IT TOOK A month to get out of my lease and make my way home, where I found the marquee that used to read *RE-OPENING SOON* down to three letters, re-arranged by the thief to *R-I-P*. The Wizard now belonged to Abe's son, Neil, who muttered something about a bulldozer when he handed me the keys. (That's how people talk in Currie:

everything's an aside.) Abe's body had been removed and buried, but no one had been back to clean. The stench was the first clue I should have run.

Instead, over the next eight weeks, I called in exterminators and cleaners and contractors to make the Wizard into a fresh two-screen split-level with new movies upstairs and rep stuff in the basement. I hired six teenagers to work weekends — selling snacks, tearing tickets, running projectors — and put money in their pockets while reducing their leisure time and ability to spend. My professors had called this "opportunity cost". We filled every seat on opening night, a Friday, and for a while six sets of parents slept easier.

HAD I KNOWN, I wouldn't have made plans. I wouldn't have let the model-making economist loose inside me, or accepted his reassurances that it's normal to lose money the first two years. I wouldn't have bought a house, or lost my shirt selling it just a year later. I wouldn't have closed the basement screen after only six months, when the jam-packed Christmas screening of *It's a Wonderful Life* was already a distant memory, and I wouldn't have eventually marked its door *PRIVATE* and lived behind it for the theatre's final weeks. I wouldn't have slept past noon every day, or eaten junk at Don's instead of healthy meals, or come back after two coffees and a fried egg sandwich just to not run the matinées no one came to.

But maybe it wasn't all my fault. Maybe it was VHS. Magnum Video opened January 1, 1985, and last time I was home, the sun-bleached *WE HAVE VCR'S!* sign was still in its window. In the end, it didn't keep teenagers in Currie any more than the new Wizard did, and already I was playing B-runs to cut costs. The kids had resumed racing to the city every weekend, their murky forms stumbling late into the Eightplex desperate for the world at the end of the light and the answer to "What's new?" —because where they were from, nothing was.

The sense that failure was inevitable sunk in on a chilly March afternoon, when I found a copy of the petition to foreclose that I had ignored duct-taped to the front doors and the handles cinched with a chain and padlock. I waited till five-to-five when the sheriff showed and I went in to retrieve what I might sell: two projectors and a popcorn maker. I didn't own a car, and I never will again, so I loaded the hardware into two shopping carts from the Price-Mart and pushed them to my parents' house, where I would have to live now. Dad bought me small For Sale ads in the *Seed-Tribune* and *Free Press*, but no one answered.

I RETURNED TO Toronto a Travis Bickle, alone after the war but with a job, at least—TD took me back, which no bank would do today for a guy with credit like mine. The city was booming at the time, and still seems to be: I've got enough work that most nights I could stay till ten, and sometimes I do before taking a long walk to the late show at Bloor Cinema. I get the subway after—west from Bathurst, last of the night—and often while I wait a work train will pass smelling of grease and hot metal and dirt. I nod to the men in coveralls and picture them at eighteen; I see myself leaving Mueller's Garage to meet Jeanie, or Scott washing up for a date with Claire, Claire who might still be in this city somewhere.

It's said that the first side of the Viaduct you live on is the one you'll stay on forever. Thirty years, more, and I haven't looked for her. I've hardly been to The Beach —the area's new name now that condos are shoving out the sparse strip—and it's too late to start going, too late to find her. I imagine the orange dress instead, the chestnut hair in the lake breeze. It's the only way I know to feel at home.

Territory

THE ANSWERING MACHINE light is blinking again and I know it's my father. He keeps after me because, too happy to think straight one Sunday after our youngest had finally started talking, I recorded, *Hi, it's Claire,* then Brad said, *and Brad,* and the boys said together *Christopher and Thomas* before we all chorused, *leave a message!* We should have left it the way it was, just the number in Brad's voice, *You've reached four-one-six ...*

At first, when Dad would just hang up, I hoped it was because he didn't recognize my voice. Two million people live in Toronto and I'm not the only Claire Burford in the phonebook. I checked.

I breathe in and press play. His monotone is measured as always.

Hi Claire, if this is you, which I'm pretty sure it is ... It's your father. Please call me.

I should have taken Brad's name.

I LEFT HOME a little more than ten years ago, 1976, which was about 1956 in Currie Township years. I had just turned eighteen and gotten my licence, and though Mom and Dad had thought sixteen too young for a girl to drive they'd had no problem letting me work the last two years, after school and weekends at the MacKinnon County Public Library in Currie. Dad would drive me in from Waubnakee on Saturdays and usually just putter around town during my shift — until the day he followed me inside and spent the four hours proving wrong something I'd said on the ride in, when we had been speeding along County Road 17 in his Nova. We were late because I'd gotten caught up in a book again.

"You'll lose your head in those things," Dad said.

"But they take you places you'd otherwise never go," I said. "There is no frigate — "

He snorted.

"What's a frigate?"

"It's a boat, Dad — there is no frigate like a book, to take us lands away, nor any coursers like a page of prancing poetry."

"You shouldn't go anywhere unless you can afford it."

My small laugh slipped out.

"This traverse may the poorest take, without oppress of toll …"

"Books are a waste of time." He took his eyes off the road and turned to me. "And time …"

I finished his sentence in a mutter: " … is money." Dad wasn't a stock trader, though, or in business of any kind. In fact, as a cop, I doubt he'd ever had reason to say this. He must have heard it on TV. I'd never seen him pick up even a magazine.

"Okay," I said. "If books are so bad, why are there so many in schools?"

"Don't know," he said, smirking. "I was never much for school, either."

"I bet you can't even read," I snapped.

He leaned over the steering wheel and narrowed his eyes. I slid toward my window. The engine's pulse quickened. He said nothing until he brought the car to a jolting stop at the library, when instead of idling and letting me out on the street he swung into the parking lot and chose an angled spot. He opened his door and slammed it and led the way to the building. As I followed him in I gave a sheepish smile to Lori-Ann, my supervisor. As usual she didn't look up from her reading, *The Collected Emily Dickinson*, again. I edged behind the counter while Dad walked to the first shelf he saw, alphabetically last but closest to the door. At random he pulled a hefty book from the middle and brought it to Lori-Ann.

"I'd like this one," he said.

She sniffed and said, "All right," then marked her place with the checkout card—a practice she discouraged among patrons. As she walked to the counter she adjusted her glasses and said, "I just need to see your library card, please."

"I don't have one," Dad said.

Lori-Ann reached beneath the counter for a form. She handed it to him. "Fill this out." Her eyes darted back to Emily.

"Why?"

She sighed. "So you can check the book out. You can borrow it for a week, and you can renew it once if no one else in the county is holding it." I stifled a laugh. Other than Lori-Ann and me no one requested specific titles

—even the schoolteachers made straight for Romance and Mystery, making off with armloads of books identical to each other right down to the full-cover author photos on the backs.

"Nah, that's okay," my father said. "I'll just read it here." He held the book up so that I could see it past Lori-Ann: *The Grapes of Wrath*. "This one any good?" he asked, too loudly. Lori-Ann swallowed hard and glanced back at me before answering.

"Yes," she said. "That's a good one."

My father leaned to one side to see past her. His smug eyes met mine.

"Well, what do you know," he said. "Your ol' Dad's not so dumb after all." He sat down at a table in the centre of the room and he stayed there long after Lori-Ann left, flipping the pages furiously until I told him it was time to shut out the lights. He was halfway through, at least. On the way home he asked if I had read it.

"Grade Eleven English," I said. "Everyone has to."

He smiled and said, "I must have missed that day."

A silent moment passed before he asked, "How's it turn out?"

"You'll have to get to the end," I said.

I DIDN'T LEAVE home because my father didn't read—I left because he started. He followed me into the library again the next Saturday and he signed up for his card and checked out *The Grapes of Wrath*. He finished it at Don's Breakfast, where I can only imagine how many times he was asked, "What the hell you *readin'* for?"

When my shift ended he picked me up and as we drove home he told me about his parents living through the Depression, and his father and his Grandpa Burford and jack drives, these mass hunts for rabbits in the woods behind their fields. Southwestern Ontario didn't seem so different than Oklahoma, he said — everyone in Currie Township planted vegetable gardens and hunted or raised the meat they needed, planning always to sell the excess though there never was any and no one had money, anyway. He exhaled at the end and said, "I wonder why my parents never went west." I looked at him as he went quiet and I didn't know what to say. "It just seems like so many people put so much into getting out there ..." He trailed off and thought a moment. "But Burfords, we just stuck around here. I mean, there must have been work somewhere we could have left for — forests up north, or mines in Quebec, or — "

"Did your parents speak French?"

"Maman did," he said. "Her family was from Pierre, you know."

"Yes, I know." *Pierre.* Another go-nowhere town along the Waubnakee River, this one settled by some Tremblays. At five hundred, its population was twice Waubnakee's. All the towns in Currie Township were shrinking as people left for London, or Toronto, or beyond, but my younger sister Susan had decided to stick around and was already working twelve-hour days at Vaughan's Bakery. Her future was sealed and mine seemed to be, too, with sixteen hours a week at the library and a promise from Lori-Ann of more when I graduated. I had the marks, but no one expected I'd go to college. The few times I mentioned it I was asked the same questions: "Since when do you need a degree to speak English?" or "What'll you do with *that*?"

In Currie Township, I read in public only in brief stretches, and usually on benches outside structures bearing Centennial plaques to commemorate the one year there was federal money, the granting program that built the ball diamonds in Waubnakee and the hockey arena in Currie and come to think of it, the county libraries, too. If someone approached, I'd say I was waiting for a ride, refuse the inquirer's offer to take me home, then race to the end of my paragraph before standing up and leaning against the wall, hiding the book in my purse and trying to look like I was just hanging out and hoping to throw off any suspicion I'd been stood up. I had found out it could be dangerous to stay in one place too long one summer night when Dad forgot to pick me up and Art Rummel, the boys' phys. ed. teacher at Currie High School, came by and offered to drive me. He insisted—*No trouble at all*—and took back roads the whole way, telling me how beautiful I had become, that I was a woman now and this town was too small for me. He lingered at every yield sign where two dirt roads met and placed his hand on my thigh, pointing out the sunset on the horizon over the nothing but farm fields. We both knew no other cars were coming, but Art stared extra long in the passenger direction anyway. It was dark when he finally dropped me off and it brought Dad to the front door, where he presumed the worst as Art's Monte Carlo pulled away. After that, suddenly, it was time I took my driving test.

LORI-ANN WAS actually waiting for someone to take her away: a visiting agricultural engineer or even a hockey dad if he were from a town where books mattered. My ticket out was Scott McLaren, who had straight dark hair almost overgrown enough for a ponytail under the battered grey ball cap he always wore and was finished high school—or finished with it, anyway—and worked for Herm Mueller, who paid him mostly in parts for his rusty VW bus. I don't remember exactly how it started with us, but Brewskie's has always been the only bar in Currie and it's always let you in well before you were of age.

We spent most of our time just riding around, and though in a lot of ways I became the new accessory for his Kraut Kan, this didn't mean I hadn't learned to drive. On the way to work at the library, Dad was my passenger now, and he followed me into the building on every trip to make increasingly flirty small-talk with Lori-Ann about Steinbeck. I had read *East of Eden* and *Cannery Row*, *Of Mice and Men* and even *The Moon is Down*, but Dad never asked me what I thought of them, he just went on and on in the car about how *well-written* the books were, an observation he was incapable of elaborating on and which didn't actually mean anything—and how would *he* know? The victory for him was just in getting to the end, book after book after book, never talking about the story or the characters or any of the things they did. Did he sympathize with them? Question their motivations? Did the story even seem believable? The whole charade was just so that I'd see him reading, or so I thought.

It got worse the day he brought home a typewriter.

THE POLICE STATION in Currie was on a corner lot, with ten parking spaces and a two-door garage. Dad's cop car had long been the only one in the township, and the second bay was occupied by Gord MacIntyre's junk shop, a heap of trinkets the poor fool had mistaken for antiques. The typewriter had sat atop the front pile for years, in plain view when the door was up — which was almost all the time — and on another crimeless day when Currie had Dad just bored enough, he bought it. He started coming home at irregular hours in the evening, stopping first for a coffee or three while he read at Don's, and after dinner he'd retire to the garage and peck away. I honestly think it was about the noise for him: a payoff for every little movement of his fingers and a counterpart to Mom's constant knitting. In her case, her half-finished sweaters were in plain view, piled ever higher beside the living room sofa and armchairs, but I never knew what Dad was writing, never even saw him bring home paper.

IT GOT TO be six-thirty, seven, seven-thirty the night Scott and I left. Dad had promised me the Nova but he hadn't come home yet. Tonight was my first turn to drive Scott anywhere, and Dad had seemed excited for me. I closed the book I was re-reading, *Huckleberry Finn*, and I got off the porch swing. I called Don's from the kitchen, and though crotchety Marlene Simmons seemed to always be at the counter, it wasn't her that picked up, but Don himself. In his raw voice he told me that Dad wasn't there. I slammed the receiver down then picked it up again to dial Scott. After that I started packing my suitcase

— Mom's suitcase — with as many clothes as would fit and of course, my favourite books.

When Scott pulled in he still wore his greasy work clothes. I climbed into the passenger seat and tossed the bag on the bench behind. I leaned over and kissed him on the mouth.

"Where are we going?" he asked.

"First, you're going home to shower," I said, touching my index to the tip of his nose. "And then, I reckon, we're lightin' out for the territory."

HUCK FINN WAS the only school book Scott had read. He was proud of it, though not as proud as he was of his van. He had never been into sports or the trivia team or students' council, and shy in all the right ways, he was an ideal first boyfriend — everything happened on my terms.

We crossed into Michigan from Sarnia and took I-75 south all night and into the next day. We didn't have much money and we didn't buy a map; we just expected we'd hit Route 66 for California somewhere. Where we finally stopped for breakfast, a dingy diner outside Knoxville, we asked the waitress and learned we were fourteen hours' drive east of the turn-off we'd been looking for. I weakened after Scott's third coffee refill and called home from a payphone. On the other end Mom's voice quivered.

"Are you all right?" she asked. "Where has he taken you?"

"I'm all right," I said.

Deep breath.

"I'm far away, and I'm never coming home."

Mom sighed.

"Well," she said. "I didn't expect you would."

Her dismissal stung.

"You know, you don't have to live there, either," I said. "Where does Dad even go in the afternoon? He wasn't at Don's last time I called—and neither was Marlene."

She exhaled and said, "I took a vow, Claire."

SCOTT AND I ran out of money in New Mexico, mercifully in Albuquerque and not on some stretch of desert road, out of gas, too. We spent the last bit on a motel room and two bottles of cheap wine, and that night we made love three times. In the morning Scott walked until he found a service station, and he struck a deal almost as good as the one at Mueller's: work till you drop, parts at cost, cash under the table.

In the motel office was a *Help Wanted* sign, so that was the job I took. We got a one-room apartment and I went to secretarial school for a while. The weather was always warm with convertibles always passing through, and their drivers whistled and yelled about my legs. Some did so with their wives in the front seat. I haven't quite dropped the weight from having Thomas yet, but Brad says I'm the same sight for sore eyes I was when, just out of med school at the University of Toronto, he checked into the Pueblo Motor Inn. He was confident he had passed his exams and was driving to Vegas to meet an old friend and celebrate. He grinned with perfect white teeth as he told me. I counted my week's pay from the till the morning he checked out, after I'd snuck away from my night shift and knocked on his door, and I handed my key ring to my supervisor before leaving in the shiny red convertible. We stopped a block from Scott's garage and I walked the rest of the way, finding him still baggy-eyed and pale-faced after waking up and finding me not home yet. He opened his arms and strode toward me but I showed my palms and stopped him. He was covered in grime.

"Thanks for everything," I said. "I won't forget it."

He tried to hide them, but tears welled in his eyes. He opened his mouth but nothing came out. I reached into my purse for my dog-eared *Grapes of Wrath* and handed it to him.

"It won't be different when you get there," I said. "Just go home."

Susan mails me pictures every Christmas of her and John and the kids, Mike and Nancy, with a letter noting somewhere near its end that Mom and Dad say hello. I call her in the morning after the boys open presents, and though they're still too young to know who they're talking to, Brad and I make them say Merry Christmas into the phone. Susan tells me all about Mom and Dad's year, and about Dad still banging at his typewriter, writing his life story or whatever. She asks if I'll get home next year and I say I'll think about it. Then I put it out of mind for three hundred days, until the phone rings and corners me again the next fall and the messages start piling up on the machine. Lucky for me, Brad closes his practice every year and takes care of gift shopping while I drink wine and ask myself why I don't just answer. When I'm about to crack I think of Dad at the library, grabbing at the bookshelf the way dogs piss on fences, and it strengthens my resolve for another year.

I know. I could call him and everything could be normal, but that would mean adopting and civilizing. I've been there before, and I can't stand it. We'd have to talk every second Sunday or once a month or something; to stop him calling all the time, I'd have to let him call all the time. Today is Thanksgiving, and here goes the phone again. I snatch up the handset and shout: "*What do you want!?*"

"It's Susan," the voice on the other end says. "I'm at Mom and Dad's." She clears her throat. "He died."

I set the receiver down. My throat lumps. My eyes burn but no tears come. Susan sounds far away.

"Claire …? Hello? Claire …? Are you still there?"

I don't say anything. Her shuffle-click-hang up takes forever. Silence, then beep, beep, beep, beep, beep, beep, beep — I re-cradle. My shoulders slacken and my jaw relaxes and I hate myself for feeling a release. I lift the receiver again and push the first digit tentatively. I gain force with each one until I pound the tenth. I hold my breath and listen to the rings. Susan answers but she doesn't speak. Her breaths are short gasps.

"So when should I come home?" I ask.

Five Stages of Sorry

THE BUNDLE IS light, ten or twelve pages at most, and tied together with old baler twine that secures a pale pink note: <u>GARBAGE</u>. Claire jerks her head back, flicking dark hair from her eyes. "The one thing Mom ever decided to throw away," she says, fanning herself with the papers and surveying the dusty junk piles in the stuffy attic. She sits down lightly on a worn cardboard box, one of what seems to be hundreds overflowing with *things*, buried under thousands of other *things*. Already we've unearthed a black trash bag worth of half-knit sweaters; most of our favourite toys; leashes for long-dead dogs. She raises her eyebrows and softens her tone to mimic Mom: "*Everything in this house is a piece of history.*"

I laugh, but my older sister hasn't been hearing Mom's voice grow frailer each day for six months like I have, since the throat cancer was diagnosed. We moved her into a hospice yesterday — Dad's been gone five years — and Claire came back three days ago, already too late to be much help. I stare at her until her eyes meet mine.

"How long has it been?"

She shifts them away from me.

"I was home for Dad's funeral."

"That doesn't count," I say. "You didn't even come into the house."

She sighs and it's as fake as her straightened hair, which I know is naturally wavy like mine. "I'm thirty-six now, and I left when I was—"

"Eighteen years."

"I wasn't welcome."

"They wanted you to come back—more than anything else."

She bends and with her free hand picks up a handful of small items from the floor: a cat ball, a thumbtack, a penny. With her fingertips she swirls them gently in her hand. "You know I couldn't, Susan. Not after what I did."

"All you *did* was leave."

"That was enough. No one's supposed to leave."

She begins flipping through the papers.

"Mom said last week not to read it," I say. "To just throw it straight out."

"Don't you want to know?" She asks, leafing some more. "I think it's a story, or something." She laughs. "What, was Mom a *writer* too?"

"I don't think so," I say.

"She loved those drugstore books," Claire says, laughing again. "Do you remember how she'd rush out the moment she heard there was a new Sidney Sheldon?" She throws back her head. "Oh, man ..."

I look over my glasses at her.

"There's nothing wrong with those books. I've read most of them, you know."

"Oh, Susan," Claire says, her voice thick with false empathy. "There's so much family drama in the plots. Are there no real bookstores out here anymore?"

"Just the rack at the Price-Mart. Danielle Steele, Robert Ludlum ... they've got quite a few."

Claire doesn't respond, stooping instead to pick up more debris: a paperclip, two pieces of miscellaneous fluff. I wish she'd throw out something that would make a difference: the seven Parcheesi sets Mom somehow accumulated; the aquarium she never got around to putting fish in; Dad's old typewriter. I look at Claire and then the bundle in her hand. "So?" I ask.

"So?"

"So what's there?"

She grins and hands it to me.

"I knew you couldn't resist."

"It's all mixed up," I say, flipping the first two sheets. "It's—"

I shriek and drop the papers. The third one is spattered with a brownish-red blood stain where the writing breaks off. Claire gathers them up. She reads silently for a moment.

"They're Dad's," she says. "Some of them are dated ... And they've all got the same title."

I step toward her and read upside down: *Apology*. She rights that page and shuffles the rest and then she says, "I think I've got them in order." She moves over on the box so that I can sit beside her, and like we did with our first Cat in the Hat books, we read.

Thursday, October 8, 1987

When Dispatch Doris radioed this morning, I was at Don's, buying two donuts and harassing Marlene across the counter. When I finally got back into the car, the garbled voice was frantic. Karen Redburn had called in news from her husband Jack and the C.B. in his combine. Doris had been trying to get me for half an hour.

My cruiser was still rolling in Karen's long laneway when she tapped the passenger window. She had on a yellow windbreaker and black rubbers, and a rooster tail stuck up from her close-cropped grey hair. This was bigger than her usual calls about drunk teenagers in the back of pickups, racing by swinging bats at mailboxes. I leaned over and unlocked her door.

"Gene Peterson's, Fourth Concession," she said, sinking in her seat. "Hurry." I turned toward the road and pulled out. She didn't say any more, which had been normal for her since her kids had left home. Sherry the Fall Fair Princess moved to Toronto to be an actress. Frederick bought a farm near Owen Sound. Asking after them was the only way to get her talking.

She mumbled, "They're fine."

"Jack okay?" I asked.

She nodded and we dropped into another silence. It lasted all the way to Peterson's, where the hundred-year-old house had been bulldozed three years ago, after Gene died and stiffed his kids — all gone to Toronto, too — by leaving the land to the Redburns to grow soybeans. You'd never know now that anything else had been there. I parked over a culvert, my car bridging the ditch, and I opened my door and stepped out. I looked back at Karen. She shook her head and didn't follow. I shrugged and lit a cigarette and waited for Jack, whose red harvester crawled along the back of the field and kicked up amber dust. As the machine drew close I thought of Gene's kids, back for the funeral, and the shock they must have had at Bartlett's Law Office when they learned they'd have no land to sell, no shared cottage to buy. Jack stifled the engine; the tines slowed to a stop. He climbed down the small steel ladder from the cab and called his usual greeting.

"What do you think?"

"About what?" I asked.

Jack squinted a moment in the sunlight. He glanced at Karen — still in the car, averting her eyes from her window — and then he exhaled loudly and stepped in front of the cruiser, where he pointed past the front tire, passenger side. With my eyes I followed his arm down to the stagnant water, where face-up James Arthur Sheehan stared back at me, two big holes in him, shoulder and gut — double barrel, vertical. I turned away and threw up. I hadn't seen a stiff in a dog's age.

"It's a murder," Jack said. "Isn't it?"

I wiped my mouth with my sleeve and nodded, thinking, "This isn't happening." The first murder out here, the Lovers' Quarrel of 1883, fills a whole wall of the Currie Township Museum, and now, three days from qualifying for my pension, I was history, too. I returned to the car and Karen covered her ears as I called it in.

"So?" Jack asked through my still-open door.

"They're sending some detectives," I said.

"From London?"

I nodded.

"So an hour?"

"Thereabouts."

"Then I can get another few rows off," he said, turning and climbing back into the combine. First the motor came to life and then, with a grinding whirr, the header. As he drove away the rumble receded to a hum. I watched for half a lap, automatic as the thresher, before I realized Karen had been scowling at me the whole time, arms folded across her chest.

"Drive you home?" I asked.

"What do you think?" she snapped.

"Not much of an apology," Claire says, ready as ever to indict Dad.

I shrug. and ask, "Who says he finished it?"

She snorts. "That's just like him — *exactly* how he apologized: heavy on the details without actually *saying* sorry." But what Claire doesn't know is that Dad became a different person after she left, and he did start apologizing — for everything, sincerely, and often for things I either didn't remember or only remembered wiping from my mind. They all felt worse the second time around. I didn't battle him the way that she did, though; the closest I ever came was the day she left home, and the You Should Have Talked Her Out Of This argument was a lot shorter than she'd like to think.

Claire stands and resumes gathering detritus from the floor.

"Where the hell was he?" she asks not to me, not to

anyone in particular. I don't know which night she means: the one where she wound up with Art Rummel grabbing at her or the one where she got into Scott McLaren's van and disappeared. I answer anyway, and catch a wistful note in my voice.

"He probably got caught up reading."

"Fuck off," Claire mutters. She looks back to the pages.

Friday, October 9, 1987

Everyone knows Sheehan did the odd job for the Hammerheads. We know he chummed around with Reginald "Merlin" Giffen, too, a long-haired kook who's lived on a side road for twenty years and fancies himself the baddest biker on the planet, writing one racist letter after another to the editor of the *Seed-Tribune* and signing them as president of yet another new "motorcycle enthusiasts' club" formed from the same selection of riff-raff and scumbags he's always run with, save for those who happen to be in jail at the time. He throws two blowouts a summer on his farm and gets his buddies fucked on the crank he cooks — the crank Sheehan bought a bit of every month to flip to college kids in London. It was double-dealing behind the Heads' backs, but mostly, they didn't care; mostly, they were up to their eyeballs in coke at Brutus's, a strip joint east of Adelaide.

The buy went down the same way on the first of every month: Sheehan would park his rusting Firebird at the ValuGas in Waubnakee, where he cashed his welfare cheque, and from there I'd follow him to the Reserve, where he'd turn off for bootleg smokes. The Rez cops didn't like us crossing the boundary, so I'd go one more block and wait in a laneway until he emerged again. I'd tail him all the way to Giffen's, where the three leaning barns were always freshly painted with the latest *M.C.* logo. Sheehan would turn in, and I'd call Dispatch and ask for Bob Moore, my superior.

A week ago, I cornered Sheehan for the eighteenth straight month. There's nothing else to do out here. "I've fucking got him, Bob," I said into the radio. "Send me out some back-up." Moore let out his usual exasperated breath and said what he always said, that Sheehan and Giffen were minnows and we should sit back, let them lead us to the bigger fish. I lit a smoke while he talked then and mouthed along with his usual parting words: "Get the fuck out of there before they spot you."

This morning, though, Moore called me at the station and tore me a new one. City Vice hadn't told him the whole story: Sheehan was deeper in with the Heads than we knew, and for the last year, had been informing in London. Moore had to yell into the phone for a long time — chain of command, shit runs downhill — but he's got nothing. I did my job per protocol and I followed his orders.

This isn't my fault, it's his.

"AT LEAST HE suggests something went wrong this time," Claire says.

"He tried, you know."

"Tried what?"

"Tried to call you," I say. "Must have been a hundred times."

"Please don't," she says, and her eyes glisten. Tears form but they don't break through. "I've moved on."

"How?"

"I made my choice," she says.

"And did you inform anyone of your choice?"

"I think he got the message."

"Claire, you didn't come home once before he died."

She stands and sniffs and walks to the window, dabbing the corner of one eye with a finger. "I couldn't have known what he was going to do," she says, looking far beyond the glass. She raises the pages to the sunlight and scans over what we just read.

"Sounds like denial," she says.

"It does," I agree, but I'm not talking about Dad.

Saturday, October 10, 1987

I can tell now, this is going to get messy. I write the following to preserve the dignity of the force: I, Constable Tom Burford, am responsible for the death of James Arthur Sheehan.

Moore said as much when he called again this morning: "Giffen sees you last week, and next thing you know, somebody at Brutus's says, 'I don't trust Sheehan.' The Heads contact Giffen — first time in years — and Giffen says, 'Yeah, I seen Sheehan, and Flatfoot with him. He's a rat.'"

Moore's right, this is on me. But today's the day. I

made my pension. I went to the bank and paid off the mortgage, and if I go before Elsa does my insurance is guaranteed, too. It only took thirty-five years. Thirty-five years and still a constable; I never was much of a cop. After a while you realize: you just need to stay long enough to retire. I wish it were under better circumstances, but effective immediately, I do.

"CONTRITION!" CLAIRE EXCLAIMS. She throws her head back and laughs.

I snatch the papers away from her.

"Honestly!" I glare and she quietens. "These are his last words!"

"Not quite," she says with a smug smile. "We're barely halfway."

"Why are you being like this?"

"Like what?"

"So insensitive. It's like nothing's going to reach you."

"Confessing he got some scumbag shot?" She scoffs. "*That's* supposed to reach me?"

"He died ashamed, Claire."

She shakes her head.

"No way. He was out anyway — he just wrote this to go cleanly. He must've been trying to keep something else hidden."

She takes back the papers and flips nonchalantly ahead.

"How can you be so cynical?" I ask.

She comes to my side.

"Look," she says.

Sunday, October 11, 1987

I shouldn't have been where I was on Thursday. I should have disobeyed Moore and stayed with Sheehan. But after we got off the radio, I drove back to Currie and parked at Don's, where Marlene was behind the counter finishing her shift, suffering Bruce Ferris as she counted her tips. He's always the last of the seed company cap-wearers to leave.

"Your other boyfriend's here," he said, winking at her. "I'd better go. Happy birthday."

He pulled the door and the bell rang.

Marlene gave the restaurant the once-over. All the seats were empty now.

"It's your birthday?" I asked.

She adjusted her greying perm and smiled, revealing her crooked incisor.

"Sure is," she said, then whispered, "the big five-oh." Her husband died twenty years ago in a tractor rollover —two years after they were married—but she kept right on, getting up with the sun every day and heading to Don's even when she wasn't on the schedule. They hadn't had children, she had nowhere else to go. With Moore clamping down, I didn't either. I still don't know why I did what I did next. I think I felt bad for her.

"Two coffees to go," I said. "I'll take you for a drive." I held the door while she carried the Styrofoam cups and we walked to my cruiser.

"You know, I've never been in one," she said.

"Not even the back?"

She dropped her jaw in mock offense. I laughed.

"Well, then. Happy birthday." I put my key in her

door like we were teenagers borrowing Dad's car, she the Fall Fair Princess (1956) and I the football quarterback (which I wasn't). I put my arm around her and peeled out even though I spend Friday nights giving teenage boys tickets for it—and never mind that I'm old and married. I've known Elsa since we were kids walking to the two-room school on Main Street, the only road in Currie at the time. She still makes us dinner every night and brews tea in her housecoat before bed, but since our girls moved out I've probably said more to Marlene than to her. It was around the time that Claire took off that Elsa quit talking. But is this why I took Marlene out in the cruiser? And why we parked on River Road outside of town and necked like we'd just left the prom? I couldn't believe it even as I did it. Marlene weighs as much as I do, maybe more, and I go to Don's for donuts every morning. My right hand was in her curls and my left was in her leggings when Doris's mangled voice interrupted.

"Tom, you've got to get out to Redburn's."

When I finally reached for the receiver, Marlene's eyes filled with pain. She adjusted her waistband and sneered.

"Get a better offer?"

In one act, I disappointed both women I'd ever been with. I took a breath and pressed the button. I waited for the beep.

I FEEL MY eyes widen as I look at Claire, incredulous.

"He changed his story—he was cheating on her!"

"Cheat*ed* on her," Claire says. "Once. And he didn't even go through with it."

"He would've."

"But he didn't."

"Wait — you're defending him?"

"It's just not that important." She shrugs. "And Mom's forgiven him, obviously. You heard her last night, calling for him in her sleep."

Mom's rasp had barely been a whisper: *Tom, we're here. We're all together. I'm coming, Tom.*

"So they got over it."

Classic Claire, washing her hands of both the issue and the debate — declaring victory by declaring fact.

Apparent fact.

Hypothesis.

"Okay, so Mom's over it," I say. "But when Dad died ..."

"Shot himself," Claire says. "The asshole."

"He was depressed! We didn't see him for days, he locked himself in the garage."

"Why didn't you go in there and get him?"

"Why didn't *you*?" I snap.

She opens her mouth but no retort comes out.

"I wasn't here," she finally says, softer.

"Of course you weren't, Claire."

She exhales before speaking again.

"So what happens next?" she asks.

Monday, October 12, 1987

Elsa wheezes while she sleeps beside me, but she's in my dreams, too, chain-smoking with half a sweater and ball of yarn on the couch beside her. She vanishes and Marlene comes next, eyes lonely as a wounded deer's while the radio squawks, and then it's Sheehan, his shaved head raining bloody pellets until his meth-mouthed wife joins him, blonde daughter on her hip as she was when she came into the station. They weep until Giffen shows, in his ratty grey ponytail, and his bushy moustache jumps as he laughs till I wake.

When Moore and I were partners—years back, in London—I arrested Giffen. He had been a Heads prospect since he was fifteen, tending bar at parties and repairing the clubhouse or sometimes helping a brother knock a woman around. I got him when he was pimping in Brutus's lot, barking at a girl a lot younger than eighteen, and I cuffed him and flopped him on the hood of our cruiser. I wanted to look tough for Bob, who had two more years on the force than I did.

Giffen looked up and flashed a shit-eating grin.

"Blueballs," he said to Moore. "What the fuck?"

With my fist I cracked Giffen on the back of his head, and when I gave him the opportunity to stay silent he said, "It'll never stick."

"Fucker's right," Moore muttered. He leaned in beside me and stood Giffen up. "We can make it stick, *Reggie*," he said, dangling the key to the handcuffs. "Or you can tell us something we want to know."

"Bob, Jesus," I said. "What are you doing?"

Giffen laughed.

"I know what you want to know," he said. He tilted his head toward the strip club. "Trisha's on tonight."

Moore smiled and said, "Take me in, then."

Onstage the women were in their forties and fifties,

stringy and saggy as those working the floor, though behind a narrow door beside the DJ booth was one exception. Giffen tugged the knob and revealed a swimsuit model blonde. Her hard-to-notice implants were barely covered by a Heads vest, black with the blue shark patch on the back. She knelt before Johnny Ragozzi ("Rags") who was long-haired, naked and filthy.

"Shit," she said. "Come back later."

Ragozzi pulled up his jeans and left the little room dangling a black T-shirt. Trisha took off the colours and tossed them to him before looking at Moore and cooing, "Hey, baby," reaching for his thigh without getting up. They shut the door from inside and left me beside the stage, alone in a peeler bar in uniform like an idiot. The bikers, easily ten of them, encircled me. A couple held pool cues higher than their heads. The music stopped, and so did the dancers. I held my breath and noticed Giffen practically salivating as he watched me sweat until the little door swung open again. Moore stepped out, flush-faced and tucking in his shirt. The bikers roared their approval.

"Giffen, you got fuckin' lucky," Moore said, pointing a finger but unable to hide the smile. "I'm coming back next week, and you're gonna tell me everything." The bar erupted in laughter. I wasn't in on the joke. We left and drove to the station, up Adelaide where drunks dotted the sidewalks. Our cruiser was the only car. It was one a.m., our shift was over. I started to ask but Moore hit the siren and floored the gas to run a red. When he turned it off I spat out, "What the hell just happened?"

He laughed.

"Arresting these little shit bikers is like Russian roulette," he said. "One in six goes off and you end up with your brains blown out." He flipped on his signal and turned into the parking lot. "Giffen's not the one," he said, killing the engine. "Scare him, make him think you'll take him down, then collect your blowjob and go home." He darkened the headlights and opened his door, letting in the cool night air. "Forget about it," he said, and the slam's echo enveloped me in the car. I sat and watched his outline all the way to his vintage Dodge Dart. The yellow beast snarled awake and Moore gunned its V8 in the street.

It could have waited till morning but I wanted my report over with, so I entered the empty station and wrote down that we had stopped at Brutus's. I listed those known to police we had seen and stared a while at the remaining white space before adding the final line: *Nothing to report.* I locked up my gun and badge, went for a leak, and then I walked to my grumpy old Nova and drove home.

All those years ago, when the Heads cut him loose, Giffen was twenty. He was an outlaw, not to mention a full-on nutbar, but he wasn't a brother. They told him that if he knew what was good for him, he'd never go near the Heads again. Moore was wrong about him, though. Giffen was the one, and the killing was his Hail Mary: the hope against hope the Heads would finally let him in.

I used to wonder why Giffen's kind took exile in Currie Township, but it's been clearer since Sheehan bought it: the place is perfect for a dead man. When Vice finally storms the farm—and they will, they're still pissed they lost a good snitch—the psycho will sing like a canary about me and Moore and Brutus's, and Moore will show them the trail back to my lie. Yeah, Moore lied, too, but like I said, shit runs downhill. He'll get a slap on the wrist, maybe a transfer back into the field. If I may, I'd like to suggest he replace me in Currie Township. It's a great place to retire.

Sheehan's death is on my head, I accept responsibility. There goes my pension, there goes my everything. But the service revolver beside my typewriter makes me smile. We've had nine-mils for years, but us older guys still call them revolvers—never mind that the mag is spring-loaded and goes off every time. It's a shame, really. Not so long ago, I was looking forward to running out the clock with Elsa.

Elsa.

I'm so sorry Elsa.

I CLUTCH THE papers to my chest. Claire wipes a tear and exhales through a slight smile. "An apology from Tom Burford," she says. "Maybe it does belong in the museum."

"We could donate it."

She shakes her head.

"Mom would be humiliated."

"It already covers half the crime wall," I say. "It was national news—"

"No way," Claire says. "This isn't important, even out here—it's just a family secret, and it's bad enough that we've seen it. Mom said to not even read it." She walks to the hole in the floor and starts down the ladder. Without looking up, she adds, "We should destroy it."

I stare after the top of her head and finally say, "You're right." I look around the attic at the countless yellowed bundles and pick one of the same thickness. Claire's old school assignments, Grade Five or so — who knows why Mom kept them. I swap them for Dad's papers before descending. At the bottom. Claire produces a barbecue lighter.

"Found it in the third drawer," she says.

I laugh.

"When in doubt …" I begin, and she smiles. Drawer Number Three is where Mom's first collections began: broken trinkets she promised to repair one day; too-short birthday candles; buttons that fell off shirts but were never sewn back on. We pass through the den toward the backyard patio. Claire slides the glass door and I walk through first. We step down from the wooden deck onto the grass.

I muster a pleading look.

"This is harder for me," I say. "It will mean more if I do it."

"If you think so." Claire hands me the lighter. I hold the sheets face down in front of me and bring the metal tip to them. I pull the trigger. Nothing.

Click.

Nothing.

Again.

Again.

On the fifth pull, it lights.

Respect

*D*AD AND I were on Highway 2, a relic of a road that detours and twists all the way from Windsor to Montreal. We were in the eastbound lane, toward London in the Buick. It was autumn, and I was eight, so he was twenty-eight.

Two's a busy road in the mornings and evenings, when those who fear the freeway drive to work in the city. You still see the odd Greyhound, but no one gets off. The company calls farm towns like Waubnakee "flag stops": if no one flags the driver, he keeps right on going.

Speed limit signs suggest ninety, to keep everyone under one-twenty, but on this Saturday afternoon the most excitement we could expect would be pulling two wheels onto the shoulder to avoid a passing combine.

Dad and I wore baseball caps, mesh-backed, consistent with local uniform. His bore a seed company logo and ensured the kids at school would keep calling my Blue Jays one a farmer hat.

Near Pierre, once a town but now just the intersection with River Road, a row of cars filled the other lane. It was half police cruisers and led by a long, low-riding black station wagon on its way to the boarded-up church and overgrowing cemetery.

Dad removed his hat and set it on the dashboard. On the horizon, one car after another materialized until the chain made the flat road appear to run downhill. He slowed the Buick a little. The hearse and the first few cop cars passed.

"It's a parade!" I said.

Dad looked away from the road.

"Get that hat off your head!"

He snatched at the peak and flung the cap into the windshield. I stared at my shoes and pretended I didn't hear the peak hit the dash with a hollow click.

I had missed my cue, and worse, I had embarrassed him, the stupid kid riding shotgun who undermined John Carrion's grand gesture.

The cap remained untouched while the entire procession passed. I didn't reach for it until Dad put his back on. He made sure to nod at me first.

I cautiously tucked my bangs under my brim.

"Always take your hat off to a hearse," he said. "To pay your respects."

I stared out the window, too scared to face him.

"But why?" I asked, so softly he didn't hear. "We're driving so fast they can't see us."

Big Man

*T*HE ALARM WAS set for five a.m., which was fine with Dad. He'd gotten up this early five days a week, twenty-six weeks a year, for three years on the swing shift at the Ritter Pulley plant. This week was one of the other twenty-six, though, and he was on the afternoon shift. After washing up and driving home to Waubnakee from Currie it was midnight before he reheated his dinner in the oven, and later yet when he wound down for bed.

Mom had waited up, which was unusual for her. She was expected at Vaughan's Bakery by seven but, unable to sleep, she told Dad what had happened that day, tiring herself out by talking. Now, it was two o'clock, and Dad's turn to lay awake and stare at the dark ceiling, wondering what to do.

It wasn't the worst problem our family had faced. My younger sister, Nancy, had earned that distinction by spending the first four days of her life feverish while our parents waited and prayed, afraid to this day that brain damage would show itself. And though my cognitive abilities had never similarly been in doubt — I learned to read before I started school — my decision-making skills were at the heart of this matter.

In my eight-year-old brilliance, I had brought a rock aboard the school bus that morning, and as Dad had taught me, planted my foot and thrown a rope to first base — one that thankfully soared high and wide of the driver, Jim Crawford, before it shattered the windshield. It forced the bus to pull off the road and made the thirty-four kids from Currie Township an hour late to our eponymous P.S. after waiting for the replacement bus to drop its teenage cargo at the high school. These were the only two buses allocated to the township, and now the damaged one sat outside Mueller's Garage, where it would wait the next week for new glass. Bus windshields weren't something Herm and his son Hank usually kept in stock.

In the interim, carpools were being set up, and we received a call from Ellen Andrews, the tobacco farm magnate's wife who was a few names above us on the phone tree and in other pecking orders. Mom listened but she declined the offer. The Carrions would deal with their own children, thank you very much. We had had enough humiliation for one day, and Mom had already bawled me out for it, slapping me a few times, which she's told me since, she regretted doing every time she did it. She finished the lecture with, "How would you like walking to school?" and this is what she recounted to Dad.

When she began to snore lightly, he set the alarm.

I MURMURED WHEN I felt the rough hands on me. It was late April, and daylight was still more than an hour away. I was sluggish and squinting in the lamplight but I noticed the heavy bags under Dad's eyes.

"Come on," he said. "We don't have much time."

"Is there a fire?"

"No. Just get ready for school."

"It's so early," I whined.

Dad smirked.

"It's a long walk."

He packed us bagged lunches — bagged breakfasts — while I put on my clothes, and we opened the door quietly, to not wake Mom or Nancy. Outside, the moon hovered low on the horizon, shimmering over just-planted soybeans in flat dark fields and carving out blocky bush outlines in the distance. Dad led with a brisk stride on the gravel shoulder while I trailed after in the ditch, kicking at the long grass. There were no cars on the county road this early, and after leaving Waubnakee's one stop sign and its blinking red eye behind, we walked in silence. My legs burned for what I now figure was ten minutes before I spoke.

"How far is it?"

"Four miles."

"Why are we doing this?"

"You know."

I met Dad's eyes.

"How much longer?"

"Depends how fast you walk."

I quickened my pace. It might have lasted five minutes.

"How many more miles?" I whined next.

"About three." Dad looked at his watch. "Time for breakfast?" I nodded and he took two peanut butter sandwiches from the paper bag. Neither of us stopped walking while he handed me one. I took a giant first bite. When we finished he fell into step behind me and unzipped my knapsack, dropping the crumpled bag and plastic wrap inside. We continued another few minutes in silence.

"Are we lost?" I asked.

Dad shook his head.

"It's a straight line. You know that. You take this road every day."

"It seems a lot shorter on the bus."

Dad smiled.

"Yeah, it does, doesn't it?"

As we walked on, pink slowly streaked the road's vanishing point, defining the contours of the woods in the distance.

"Wow," I said. "I've never seen the sun rise."

"You've got to get up pretty early," Dad said.

"DAD? I'M TIRED," I said.

"It's not far now."

"You said that twenty minutes ago."

"It wasn't twenty minutes," Dad said. He checked his watch again. "It was five," he lied.

"Feels like forever," I said.

We were halfway there and it was nearly seven. Dad knew a man could walk a mile in less than twenty minutes, and because I was younger with energy to burn, he must have counted the same for me. After all, he'd done it often in his teens, walking home from Currie's pool hall when he ran out of quarters, regardless of the hour of day or night, from the time Grandpa Ralph learned Dad wasn't on the volleyball team until the day Dad got his driver's licence. It was a young Jim Crawford that had gotten Dad his ride every morning, though, and when he stopped the bus at the high school, he would say to Dad, "Make sure you go inside today." Dad would agree, but as the bus smoked away he'd survey the parking lot for someone he could challenge to cut class and play nine-ball against him for cigarettes.

It was daylight now, and I was still complaining. Dad lit his first of the day.

"Don't tell your mother," he said.

I FELT THE burning in my legs first, and next in my back. We'd been walking two hours, and now in the cerulean sky Currie's flour mill and its one apartment tower had come into silhouette.

"Look, Dad! Look!"

"Yep. Gettin' close."

"How much longer now?"

The burning climbed into my lungs.

"A few more minutes. Just keep walking."

"I can't," I said, and I plopped down on my seat in the damp grass.

"What do you mean? We're almost there."

On the county road, more cars headed out of Currie toward London, speeding up near the town limit sign and forming a rapid river. Commuters had whizzed by indifferent to us the dark, but in daylight now some rubbernecked to our standoff in the ditch. Vehicles going the same direction as us passed less often, mostly pickups with a few tractors mixed in, but all had room for two more passengers and so did Curt Andrews, the baron himself. He pulled over and idled his Cadillac.

"John Carrion!" he shouted out the window. "You boys need a ride?"

I jumped up.

Dad shook his head.

"We're walking today."

Andrews laughed and said, "Suit yourselves," pushing the switch. His window slid shut and I watched him drive away until he turned onto Main Street. I climbed out of the ditch and walked to the rusty wire fence, where I sat with my back against it and began to cry.

"Stop that!" Dad yelled. "You're a big man now."

"I'm only eight!" I blubbered. I wiped tears with my cuff. "I'm not, Dad. I'm not a big man."

"You thought you were when you threw that rock."

"But I didn't do it! Patrick Andrews did!"

I put my hand to my mouth, too late to catch the words.

"What?" Dad said.

I covered my eyes and cried louder.

"He said he'd beat me up if I told."

Dad's brow furrowed. He sat down beside me. Above us, two buzzards circled and cawed.

Dad said, "Something must have died here." He stood and looked left. Looked right. Down the fenceline, in the ditch, was a raccoon killed by a car. I rose and followed as Dad approached the carcass, its sides split, spilling organs. A white bone jutted out, picked clean.

"Do you know where our name comes from?" Dad asked.

"It's French."

"But do you know what it means in English?"

"Carry on?" I asked.

Dad looked up from the roadkill. The school was ten minutes yet, even with me in tow.

"Sure," he said.

I sniffed. The tears had stopped.

Dad squatted and put his hands on my shoulders.

"You ready, big man?" he asked.

I nodded.

"Let's go," he said.

Bondo

The navy Chev pickup waited on Ed Donlon's lawn on the concession road under a cream-coloured topper with short, wide windows. Rust blisters had broken all around the wheel wells, and elsewhere more bubbled beneath the paint. The black sign in the windshield read *FOR SALE* in orange, with *$1,000* markered beneath.

Dad parked our brown Buick, the paint so salt-worn it looked like chocolate with the nibs in, and left my sister Nancy and me inside with the windows rolled down. It was a Saturday in May and already hot.

We heard a sputtering small engine and then, "John Carrion!"

Donlon appeared from behind the brick house, shirt open, reclining on a green lawn tractor with a beer can between his thighs. He reached down and shut the blades off before the gravel laneway, and when he got to us he reefed on the handbrake.

"What brings *you* here?" he yelled over the engine. Leaning forward, he turned off the key, smiling as he reclaimed his sweaty beer. He swiped it under the brim of his fishing hat. "You wouldn't be looking for a previously enjoyed ve-*hick*-le, would you?"

Dad said, "Well, yeah. That's exactly what I'm here for."

As he and Donlon talked the car's interior heated up. Nancy opened her door, like always. I was ten, she was seven, and when she let in more air I thought she looked stupid—especially when she did it on Main Street in Currie while we waited for Mom to run errands. I told her to shut it but she pretended not to hear me, like we pretended not to hear Dad and Ed.

"That asshole Hank Mueller was out," Donlon said, referring to the *Owner and Proprietor* emblazoned on the doors of the one tow truck in Waubnakee. "He thinks she needs a new motor. Says he's got one in the back of the shop, too."

He lit a cigarette.

"Offered me five hundred bucks."

"What'd you tell him?" Dad asked.

"I told that sonofabitch to get the fuck off my property."

Donlon laughed at himself, proud and wistful at the same time. He took a swig from his can.

"This old truck's been going good fifteen years now," he said. "She deserves more respect than that."

Dad furrowed his brow and looked over his safety glasses. In his best Hard Man Voice he said, "Is eight respect enough?"

Donlon shook his head.

"Thousand *safetied*," he said.

"Eight hundred," Dad countered. "I'll get the road test myself."

Donlon looked back at the house. His new Silverado series was parked in front of the garage.

"Well, you need her more than I do," he said. "Sure. We got a deal."

Donlon and Dad shook on it. Nancy shut her door. It blew our cover but it closed the transaction. Dad said we'd be back later and we drove off.

After work at the bakery Mom was tired that night, but she got in the car with us, floury clothes and all. Donlon was drunk when he answered the door, but he took the money and handed over the keys. Dad opened his door and I climbed in, scooting across the bench seat before he lowered the shifter and let out the clutch.

FOUR MONTHS PASSED before Dad got started. By then, the rust holes were as big as my fists, but the truck was the second job that summer; first, we had to clear the garage so he'd have somewhere to work. We did it on a Saturday and left just enough for Sunday to avoid going to church with Mom and Nancy.

In the debris was a piece of plywood Dad claimed he'd long been looking for. We painted a red square on it and attached my hoop from two Christmases ago, mounting it finally to the front of the garage. I was years from making any three-pointers, four feet tall and sixty-three pounds, but still I took one side of the chest freezer that hadn't run in years and helped Dad hump it out to the road. We dropped it next to old bottles that had been on the windowsills when we moved in, and the tricycle Nancy was too old for, and the cage for Mom's budgie that died the week I was born. We hadn't used these things in years but we inexplicably clung to them.

Waubnakee wasn't—still isn't—like Toronto, where my Aunt Claire says salvageable garbage disappears from the curb in the time it takes to make coffee. Our heap waited all week for Thursday night pick up, and thanks to Currie Township's arcane bylaws it was still there the next weekend. The truck's last trip before it came off the road was to the dump, to toss the junk.

When we returned Dad reversed up the laneway. I got out and stood at the back of the garage, waving in his mirror, leaving him three feet so he could get around the truck when he worked on it. He grazed the side wall when he opened his door and then he edged past the hood. In the laneway we looked back at the vehicle's nose. It protruded from the doorway like the toes out Dad's sock holes. We put paper in the orbital sander, his own unused Christmas gift, and he led the fight against the rust's ragged fringes. I followed with a sheet of extra-fine, buffing the gristly steel into naked, toothless planes.

DAD HAD WORKED at Ritter three years, sorting fan belt pulleys in Quality Assurance. One whole paycheque covered the truck, and once he bought it, a bank loan covered us. To pay it off he switched to graveyard for the premium—fifty more cents an hour, like it would have made a difference. He picked me up in the Buick one day after school and took me to the plant to show me around. Day Shift Leon sat on the stool at Dad's work station, and when Dad tapped his shoulder the beefy man shrugged and grunted, taking a pack of smokes from his rolled-up blue sleeve and wandering off.

Dad bent and lifted an empty bin from the floor. On the tabletop he started filling it with to-standard parts, flinging bent or burred ones in a receptacle at his feet. I couldn't hear them clunk through my earplugs when they landed, but under borrowed steel-toed shoe covers I felt the concrete floor vibrate. I watched for an hour. New pulleys came every seven minutes.

Night shifts should have given Dad more time for the truck. When he woke in the afternoon he could have cranked classic rock and spent the day sanding in the garage. But not long after we took the licence plates off, Dad found he couldn't keep up at work. He came home in the mornings with his right wrist swelling and met me and Nancy in the kitchen, where we'd be making lunches. Squeezing in beside us he'd take an icepack from the freezer then retire to the bedroom for the day.

Later, when he was on Workers' Comp, he could have even slept nights and worked days on the truck if not for the orbital, which sent shockwaves through his ulna like a cracked bat and a foul ball. He endured it for a weekend to show me how the tool worked, and after pointing out the kill switch he asked me to lead, following with a sanding block in his good hand.

In a month we had all the rust smoothed. Dad beamed as he explained that Bondo was the next step. We mixed the putty and the hardener in a cut-off bleach bottle and the acrid smell stung in my nose. Dad trowelled the compound over the holes on the back fender but conceded before he reached the tailgate. Fine movements were too much now, too.

From then on, there the truck sat. Snow drifted around

it and into the garage, piling up along the side walls while outside, the stripped front end grinned like a skull with headlight eye sockets, a bottom lip bumper and a nasal cavity where the bowtie had been. It stared me and Nancy down every afternoon when we got home from school and taunted Dad deep into the winter.

IN MARCH, AFTER months of meetings and hearings, Ritter paid Dad a settlement. Sixty days' wages. Not quite three thousand dollars.

Even Nancy and I knew it was an insult. It was also the most money our family had ever seen at once. A chunk of it went down on the mortgage, I hope, and Nancy and I got some new clothes. But the money didn't solve our problems, it made them worse. Mom and Dad fought for a week straight, deep into the night, and though I could barely make out words from my bedroom, I knew it was about the money. Lately it always was. Short of staying in Waubnakee and pumping at ValuGas, the one workplace in town, Dad couldn't get a job without a vehicle. He wasn't thirty yet, but when he yelled *"It's my fucking arm, so it's my fucking money!"* I knew he felt too old to go back to being a pump monkey.

That Saturday, he asked me to help him put the truck's lightbulbs back in. The four-ways clicked the whole way to the drive shed at Grandpa Ralph's, where we met Dad's brother Richard, who had won his high school auto shop award every year and who didn't like to come to Ralph's unless he absolutely had to. Dad offered some of the money, though, maybe the last of it, and Richard accepted.

BY SUMMER'S END Richard had the truck back on the road, pale blue and minus the topper. Dad was so proud. On weekends he took it out "just for a drive," he helped friends move when they didn't even need it, and though we never had more than would fit in the cab, he always put our groceries in the back. We got a lot of attention around town, especially from our closest neighbours, Steve and Dana, the young couple across the tracks with three kids of their own.

"I see your Dad got his truck back," Dana said, prying subtly at me and Nancy at the ValuGas where the school bus stopped. She waited for us to fill the silence: to hear that Dad's licence suspension was over or the repo hadn't gone through or something. Kids say the darnedest things.

Hank Mueller noticed, too, and made sure to tell his daughter Jessie, who was the same age as me and already growing breasts. On the school bus she'd play with a strand of long black hair and say, straight-faced, "My Dad's going to buy your Dad's truck." Not knowing it was hopeless, I'd snap back, "It's not for sale, you bitch!"

And it wasn't. For once we were doing fine. Comp had cleared Dad to take a new job in London that started with three weeks of seminars about life insurance. He came home after dark those nights and we had dinner so late that Nancy and I had to go straight to bed afterward

—and because her shifts started so early, so did Mom. Dad stayed awake at the kitchen table and practiced his pitch with his new tape recorder.

DAD'S CREDIBILITY WAS instant, so much so that his sales were sixth in Canada that November. He set his appointments weeks in advance, and instead of gliding up in a Japanese city coupe, he bumbled around in the baby blue pickup, now almost *officially* a classic. Sceptical, and seeing Dad on ultimatums from their wives, husbands were immediately impressed; in an hour, chit-chat about the rare seventy-four short-box turned into another sold policy.

At the time there were fifteen thousand people in Currie Township. A few were long-term farmers with no plan to speak of—crop insurance, sure, but *life?*—and the rest were retirees from the city, who had graduated back when Western students stuck around and had paid into London Life since.

Of course, London Life wasn't who Dad worked for. His company was American Life Insurance Inc., whose TV ads sang "We spell *ally* A-L-I-I" at night when the Cleveland stations fuzzed in across Lake Erie. Dad's job was to make people switch.

Before long our new answering machine was overloaded with messages. It was bad enough to learn that an acquaintance had died, but what was worse was that the calls weren't about that. Caller after caller told of unpaid claims and begged, "Jesus, John. Isn't there *some*thing you can do?"

There wasn't. And once it got around that Dad was part of a scam — a scam he hadn't recognized, and still didn't — ALII gave him a new territory called Pill Hill: Highway 4 north of London, where the city's doctors lived in mansions.

Dad was excited, at first. There was money to be had. But instead of meeting quarry in the laneway like he had in the township, in London Dad had to ring doorbells. When they answered, if they answered, clients took one look at his ve-*hick*-le — the *old* truck that he drove — and right away the sale was off.

Thankfully, Nancy and I had our new school clothes, because that winter even Dad's yearly deer hunt didn't fill the freezer. A lot of nights we praised the versatility of Kraft Dinner — it wasn't even KD, it was Price-Mart store brand, but it really did go with everything.

EASTBOUND ON 401, a Friday morning in the spring, the truck began to clatter. Dad was in the fast lane and pushing too hard, rushing to make his first appointment. Lately he always was. By then he'd started smoking again, which Mom and Nancy didn't know at the time. I imagine he tossed his butt out the window and weaved urgently to the centre, the right, the shoulder, stopping then resting his head on the steering wheel. And though I don't want to think it, he probably cried. From there he walked the three miles to J's Truckstop and called the one wrecker he knew. Hank Mueller stopped his orange tow truck an hour later and readied the winch on the yellow boom.

"*Shit*, John. What happened?"

"Well, first it ticked ... then it whirred, faster and faster ... and then ... it kind of clunked," Dad said.

Hank popped the hood for a look. He closed it right away.

"You're in trouble," he said, complete with a head shake and a look to the ground. "You threw a rod. She'll never run again." Dad says Hank's eyes gleamed like a wolf's: teeth bared and bloodthirsty, claw at the ready. "Hundred bucks for 'er, John. On the hook," he said. "Won't even charge you the tow."

I want to say Dad just glared back and spat, but he probably sighed and said nothing. They took the slow way home, crammed onto Old 22 westbound, and when they got back to Waubnakee, Dad paid with the last bit of room on his credit card. He asked to use the phone with the grimy receiver.

Nancy and I had our lunches made and were nearly out the door when we heard the ring. I told her to turn down the black-and-white TV in the kitchen. She insisted on leaving it blaring when we left, so burglars would think we were in.

"Is your mother there?" Dad asked. He *never* used mother.

"She went to work," I said.

"In the car?"

"She walked. She said she'd save the gas."

He breathed in.

"Okay," he said. Exhaled. "The truck broke down."

He paused a moment, and then he hung up.

I was shooting baskets the next Saturday when Hank's wrecker growled behind me. He blew the horn and I forgot about my ball, letting it plonk off the Buick's side door.

Hank's hands were oily and he hadn't shaved. He had to have just come from a job. He took the cap off his head and ran two fingers through his comb-over. He spat in the laneway.

Dad had slept late. He emerged in an old T-shirt and sweatpants.

"You drive a hard bargain," Hank said. "Not returning my calls."

Dad flinched, but then he stared back. Right into Hank's eyes.

"I told you. It's not for sale."

"Fine, Joan," Hank grunted. "Five hundred. *As is.*"

I looked up at Dad, gaping. He looked down and his eyes begged.

I nodded.

I was twelve now.

Dad raised his head and whooshed.

"Deal."

Tabaco Babies

*T*OWNIES' LITTLE BROTHERS get it first. That's why I scurry into the room panting, late for my first Grade Nine class. Everyone stares as I skulk to the back, where I take a seat between two boys. On my right, one whispers an introduction.

"Mike Carrion."

"Brian Callaghan," I mumble back, looking up at my gangly new friend. Way up. Mike's from a township school, but just like in prison — where they'll be in three years — the seniors picked him because he's tall. His left eye is swollen and already turning purple, and his forehead reads *looser* in faded blue marker. The skin is still red from scrubbing.

Boys know what to expect from Currie High School. And though Mike got it bad, initiation's even worse for girls; most of them think they're safe because they're *nice*, or in figure skating, or their dad owns a big tobacco farm, but it just makes them bigger targets. Senior girls have *skank* and *whore* and *slut* at their disposal, and when they catch a Ninerette they pen them all on her in looping, perfectly-spelled cursive. A ball-point hurts more than a marker, and for some girls it never wears off.

On my other side is a short boy named Ben. I know him from fastball. He's not bruised like Mike, but his knapsack is torn — a casualty of his getaway, no doubt. On his T-shirt, a yellow stain is still wet.

They egged him. Until now I thought that one was made-up.

Mrs. Kulich clears her throat. She taught my parents Grade Nine math, and already, I can tell: she'd rather be our mother than our teacher. It's like the first day of kindergarten but worse. She asks, "Did anyone have trouble finding the classroom?" and peers out the red frames under her grey bob. I think she expects us to answer.

Yes, me. I was running from these seniors, see, and I wound up in the shop hall, and these guys with mullets and backwards ball caps with pot leaves on them —

No. No one's going to say that, on the first day or any other.

"Well, then. Let's get started. The first thing I have is the seating plan."

Everyone groans. We thought we had left those in Grade Eight.

Mrs. Kulich backpedals.

"It's only for the first month," she says. "Just until I learn your names."

She looks around the room. No one admits to caring. She points to the front left corner and the desk face-to-face with hers.

"So ... in alphabetical order. Can I have Benson Allen here, please?"

Front row, centre, two girls gasp. One's a blonde in pigtails and the other has a long brown braid. They clearly chose these seats thinking grades make you popular. Pig-Tails' braces flash. She's going to need a couple of years.

"Hello, Benson," Mrs. Kulich says when Ben sits down. "And behind him, can I have … Kimberly Andrews?"

The brunette looks at Pig-Tails and hesitates before getting up. For a moment I expect them to touch hands, like inmate and visitor through glass on a cheesy TV show.

"Come on, Kimberly," the teacher says. "There's nothing to be afraid of."

Everyone in the room cringes. We know what she's going to say next.

"He's not the same as us, that's all. No better or worse, just … *different*."

Kimberly gathers her pink pencil case and knapsack. She shuffles to the desk behind Ben, which her brother Pat's burly best friend Ryan Tern has staked out. When Ryan stands he says to Kimberly, "Better you than me," louder than even he thinks. His steel toes clomp to the desk beside Pig-Tails. Ryan has two years and thirty pounds on all of us. No one says a word. Not even Mrs. Kulich.

THE WORST THING the seniors can write — or spell — is *Fag*, but that one washes off pretty easily. In Currie, everyone's straight. And everyone's white, too. Well, almost. The tobacco farms hire workers from the Caribbean, mainly Jamaica, and four or five times a summer, you'll see a picker cycling on the shoulder of the county road, usually on his way to the Price-Mart for cigarettes. My older sister Stella worked there as a cashier under the usually pointless *We I.D. under 25* sign. Earlier this year, three Jamaicans came in, and Stella got fired for carding them.

"Are you kid-*din*'? Twenty-five? We are *past* it," one man insisted.

Stella was sure they were old enough, but her manager was standing right there. She had to ask. Had to dig in when they refused.

"Sir, I'm sorry," she said. "I can't sell you cigarettes without I.D."

"I come here and pick you' tobacco *five years now*, and I can't buy it wit-out you axin' *I-D*?"

That's where the manager stepped in.

"Just give them to him, Stella," he whispered. "Don't be a hero."

BEN AND I were opponents every summer until this one, when we both made Currie Blue, the stacked team in our age group. Ben's the backup catcher behind our captain Chad Mitchell, and I'm the second-best pitcher. We got to know each other well on the bench, and after practice on Fridays we'd walk home together, through the alley behind Main Street. Passing the quiet back doors to Darla's Flowers and Currie Home Video, our conversations would echo to the end of the row and drown in the racket behind Brewskie's: *The Only Bar in Town*, just like the sign says, with *Only* underlined in case you didn't get it. The sign out front could say anything, though; Brewskie's is the kind of place where you're only cool if you use the back door. It's also the other place you might see a picker. Most times when we approached we'd see Ryan and

Pat, already drunk and hassling the bouncer. We'd crouch behind a dumpster and watch an exchange like this:

> PAT: You've *got* to let us in.
> RYAN (*nodding aggressively and leaning in*): Yeah!
> (*Marty shifts uncomfortably.*)
> PAT: Come *on*, Marty. Can't let the spooks at our girls.
> RYAN (*louder*): Yeah!

The two would tower over him while a line-up formed behind, chanting *Mar-ty's a ho-mo* until the pudgy doorman exhaled heavily and scanned the alley for a cop. The cop. Currie only has one. When he was finally sure Bob Moore was nowhere in sight, Marty would hustle the two of them inside.

BEN CAUGHT THREE games the week Mitchell and his family were at the lake. His throws to second were solid, and the pitch calls were smart, but the problem was his bat. At our first practice with Mitchell back, Coach Little told Ben he was done for the season.

That was the first night we stayed late at the diamond. Ben had it in his head that he'd prove everyone wrong. I threw to him until eleven, when the floodlights clanged off, and then we walked home through the alley, which had filled with seniors while we trained. They clustered around Pat, who hovered over a kneeling Jamaican. The man had to be in his forties. Ben and I took up our positions.

"That's *our* money, Picker," Pat said. "And we say you don't spend it here."

He drove his fist into the migrant's teeth. The man fell to the ground, where he cowered and turned out his palms. Pat wiped the blood on his jeans.

"Please," the man begged.

Pat snorted.

"Had enough already? No wonder you can't get a job in Ja-*may*-ca," he taunted, drawing it out in an un-Jamaican accent. He leaned forward and spat out a nicotine-yellow gob. It stuck in the worker's eyebrow. Pat cocked his fist to swing again.

Marty caught the arm and twisted it behind Pat's back, growling, "That's enough!" He looked down the alley. "Get out of here before Moore shows up."

Pat broke free of the bear hug and he and Ryan took off down the alley. They cut through the Price-Mart parking lot and vanished down Main Street over Memorial Bridge, so low to the Waubnakee River that when you're dared to jump, you have to. The crowd dispersed and Ben and I crossed the lot, too. We were nearly to my street when Moore's squad car finally screamed past.

I ASKED BEN once what had happened with his father.

"He left, I guess. I don't know," he said. "It just didn't work out."

In Currie, that's not saying much. A lot of marriages don't work out. Ben's parents are just among the few that did anything about it. Splitting up here is tough because right away, everyone finds out, and worse, they tell everyone else why it's happening, regardless of whether they actually know. I'd bet the decision was easy for Ben's mom and dad, though. Anything would be, compared to walking down Main Street feeling the stares: Mom White, Dad Black, Baby Benson somewhere in between.

"Every year, *some*one falls for a picker," Stella told me once. She may not have much to go on — she's only sixteen — but she's been going to Brewskie's every weekend for a while now. I sneak out some Saturdays and meet her for a cigarette in front. I don't tell Mom Stella's not at Jessie Mueller's house, and Stella doesn't tell that I smoke.

"It's usually a fat hick who works at the plant," she said, "but every once in a while, it's a young girl who's going somewhere." A bitterness crept into her voice. "Someone who might get out of here one day."

She lit a second cigarette.

"The girl ends up head over heels, and starts thinking they'll be the ones. That *this* time, for *this* couple, things will be different. But they never are. The man goes home when the season ends, before the girl even knows she's pregnant, and then she gets to decide. She drives into London for an abortion, or she has the baby and hopes for the best."

"The best?" I asked.

Stella swept her drooping blonde bangs off her forehead.

"For the guy to never come back," she said. "The girl lays low until the baby's born, and then she tells people it's adopted or a nephew or something."

She pursed her lips and turned away, blowing the smoke out her nostrils.

"Look around. There are only four black kids at our school. Jeez, you're friends with one of them. Nephew Ben. Have you ever seen *his* parents?"

Anger welled up in my eyes. I flipped her the bird and stormed off down Main Street, unsure what upset me more — that she had said Ben came from Minute Rice and pancake mix, or that she was right about there being no black families in Currie.

Coach Little had been true to his word, but Ben said my pitches were helping. We stayed late every week, and afterward, we watched the fights. All that ever changed was the victim.

The last week before school, Pat chose a picker who was around thirty-five, six-foot and bulky from a summer in the kilns. The man held his own until Ryan jumped in; now, he lay on the ground. The attackers rained kicks on his sides and taunted, "Leave our women *alone*," as he rolled and tucked, absorbing the blows. Between an on-looker's legs his eyes implored us to do something but we darted back into the dumpster's shadow, terrified that our cover was blown.

Ben whispered, "That's my dad."

"No way," I said.

Ben peeked around the corner.

"No, it isn't. I don't think. But it could be." He looked at the sky and let out a weighty breath. "I can't wait until they let me inside."

Pat took the worker by the collar. He lifted him to his knees and smashed his nose with a left. The seniors cheered.

I tugged the shoulder of Ben's jersey.

"Come on. Let's get out of here."

Our cleats drubbed like hail on the asphalt. I didn't think they heard us run off.

THERE ARE TWENTY-FIVE desks in the classroom. I already know I'll be sixth. Mrs. Kulich calls Matthew Bartlett —lawyer's kid, he's such a dork—and then the pompous Brown twins, Jake and Gary. I'm on my feet before I hear my name. Ryan vacates my new desk, and on the way by he makes sure to brush me hard with his shoulder.

Mrs. Kulich smiles and carries on. Mike's next, then Pig-Tails. Her name is Megan Cavanagh. Her desk creaks when she sits, and right away, loose-leaf ruffles. She passes a folded paper to Kimberly, who drops it over Ben's shoulder. I see Ryan nod in the back row, eyes shining with way more anticipation than waiting for last names beginning with T requires.

Ben unfolds the note.

YOUR DEAD TABACO BABY.

He looks up at Kimberly.

"Ryan Tern," Mrs. Kulich says, groaning. The ox looks up with a goofy grin. I hold my breath. Maybe she saw. She checks the seating plan and breaks the order to give Ryan his permanent spot now, in row four.

Ben crumples the note. He drops it on the floor. Kimberly retrieves it.

"That's so racist," she whispers.

Ben replies, "No, it isn't."

Ryan lurches right and thunders into his new seat. He

takes a penknife from his jeans and starts marking his territory, carving his name in the wood. He looks up when Mrs. Kulich starts the lesson, averting his eyes to scowl at Ben instead.

That's you, Ryan mouths. *Tobacco Baby.*

Ben returns the stare.

Takes one to know one, he mouths back.

Eyesore

A FEW SUMMERS AGO it wandered up to my grandparents' farm, burrs in its red and gold fur and stinking of pond water. It looked like a Retriever or a Collie to Grandma Anne, and she had a feeling it was older, and female. It sniffed around the old barn while she yelled girls' names from the porch. It came running at "Lucy," so that's what Grandma called her.

Called *it*. When you write, you call a dog *it*. "It" would have been a fine name. "It" looked like an Addams Family cousin. But Grandpa Ralph, he had other names for Lucy, secret ones like "Bitch" and "Cunt" he used when Grandma was out of earshot.

See? It's important she's a she.

After Christmas last year, Grandma told Ralph she never should have quit school to marry him and she moved home to Edmonton. She met a Russian doctor with a collection of inoperative antique rifles on his walls there, but that's not what this story's about.

IT'S THREE-THIRTY IN the afternoon. I'm just off the bus from Currie High School, Grade Nine, and I barrel through the front door to answer the ringing phone.

"Mike, hi. It's your Grandpa Ralph."

He starts every call this way—never just *Grandpa*, never just *Ralph*. His next question is always the same, too.

"Is your Dad there?"

"No, he's at work," I say.

Grandpa Ralph says he'll call again later and hangs up. He's always forgetting that Dad's back on afternoons at Ritter, arm swelling again and an MRI in London still a month away. Ralph forgets because to him, "at work" is all-or-nothing: he goes away for months at a time on the oil pipeline in Alberta. No one understands why he hasn't just moved there. Growing up in Currie Township is no reason to stay. Ralph's left every spring since before Dad was born, and returned every fall when the ground out west has frozen, finding children, now grandchildren, taller and tanned after spending the summer cutting grass and tending to his oversized garden and his fruit trees for the pickles and pears and apples and cherries Grandma Anne used to spend every August sealing in Mason jars.

A long time ago, before Dad quit drinking, he wobbled out to Ralph's in his roaring Olds Cutlass and started a Boy-Named-Sue fight about these summers. Grandma Anne screamed from the porch while father and son rolled in the dirt laneway like school kids, stopping only when Mom's Uncle Frank happened by in his truck and broke it up. He loaded Dad into the box and drove him back to town, or so I heard years later—I didn't see it, I was asleep in my crib. Mom says that even Dad kicking in the screen door didn't wake me.

LUCY. SHE STARTED as an outdoor dog, but on cold winter nights Grandma would open the back door and let her in, wiping the snow from her paws with an old towel. And even after Grandma left, until the spring, Lucy spent most nights in the house, where I would pat her belly and ruffle her fur as I lay beside her on Ralph's living room carpet, on my stomach with the newspaper's sports page spread in front of me while Ralph in his recliner ranted along with Coach's Corner, Dad agreeing from the couch.

Since making his amends way back, before I started kindergarten, Dad's been Ralph's best friend. They go deer hunting every November, and in the winter they make me help cut wood for Ralph's stove, which means standing around in the bush behind his farm freezing my toes while they run chainsaws and yell at me to pick up the logs and load them into the old wagon attached to Ralph's burgundy Massey-Harris.

As I scratched behind Lucy's ears on a Saturday night just before the playoffs this year, Ralph said, "Be careful. You let a woman in once," but he trailed off. Dad laughed, then caught himself, as though he'd just remembered I was there.

THE BUS FROM Currie Elementary trails blue, oil-burning smoke as it passes the house, having just unloaded Nancy and some other kids at the ValuGas. When she gets home we watch *Y&R* at four and make fun, and then it's the *Simpsons* rerun at five before we start on the chore list Mom always leaves. It's like a game, seeing how long we can put it off before we lunge across the finish line.

Nancy's job is dishes and mine is the vacuuming. That's why I don't hear the kitchen phone ring. It startles me to see her in the doorway between the dining and living rooms, tears on her cheeks under her glasses and arms limp at her sides. Dishwater drips from her hands.

"What?" I ask. "What is it?"

"Grampa said, 'I need you to be a secretary,'" she says, which is Ralphspeak for "take a message" when someone's daughter picks up. "He's going to work tonight," she starts. "He called from the airport—" She collapses into my chest, sobbing and unable to talk.

The pipeline's so dangerous that it has to pay well; no one would take the jobs, otherwise. Ralph's cheated death for more than thirty years. He has the money to retire, and he's barely fifty. His whimpering secretary is ten-and-a-half. "He can't keep Lucy," she blubbers. "He said to remind Dad to ..." She sniffs. "To shoot her, and bury her behind the shed."

Louder sobs, and a widening wet patch on my T-shirt. I hug her close to me. The rug stays half vacuumed, the dishwater goes cold, and a minute later we hear Mom's brown Buick crunch the laneway gravel. Its engine dies. Her keys jingle. The door opens. She looks at the vacuum, its hoses still strewn about. She adjusts her glasses and eyes me, then Nancy, then me again. When our chores aren't finished, she knows why. She sighs.

"What were you fighting about?"

She's been working at the bakery since early this morning. Her curly blonde hair is frizzing and purple bags underline her wire-rims.

"We weren't fighting," I say, and because we didn't chorus, "Nothing!" she believes us.

Nancy, on the couch now, looks down at our cat, nestled in front of her under the coffee table. It—she—jumps to her feet and breaks for a bedroom down the hall. I explain to Mom in the shortest way possible. Nancy starts crying again anyway.

"I don't think so," Mom replies. "I don't think so." She turns back to the door where her keys are still in the lock. She removes them. "Nancy, we'll be right back," she says. "Put on your shoes, Michael."

UNTIL RALPH HAD it torn down four years ago, Lucy lived inside the old barn. After dinner every night, Grandma would walk up the laneway with two small Rubbermaids, one filled with Lucy's food and the other with chow for the umpteen stray cats that came and went and often left kittens. Ralph complained about how much Grandma spent on kibble, and threatened to drown the cats—"For their own sake," he said—but after the demolition crew finished, he and Dad cut up the timbers and filled in the pond where I learned to fish and skate; whole Currie Township generations played shinny here, dawn to dusk on weekends. The cats have run off and now there's just more grass for someone to cut—me, for a hundred bucks a summer. Dad calls out west if I miss even one Sunday, saying, "We can't have it looking like an eyesore," and then Ralph says the same to me a day or two later, over the phone from some place with a name like Carrot Creek.

Ralph paved the laneway, and years ago, just after Dad moved out, he tore down the house my great-grandfather had built way back when the barn held cattle. He replaced the house with a sprawling one-storey: three bathrooms, four bedrooms, and now, only him to sleep there. The barn made way for the aluminum drive shed for the Winnebago he and Grandma were going to buy, but it sits mostly empty now, always locked. The whole property looks modern except for the doghouse, which Ralph says Grandma insisted on buying for summers, when Lucy lived outside. The rusty tin roof makes me think he got it second-hand, and probably at the Currie Township Dump. This eyesore must not count.

The dog barks as we drive in and pulls her chain taut from its steel stake. Mom nudges the car along the laneway. As we round the loop that circles the drive shed, we see the metallic green nose of Dad's Cutlass peeking out from behind. It's still strange to see the car anywhere but on our lawn — after selling the truck, Dad and Richard spent a whole year of weekends redoing the muscle car's brakes, suspension, exhaust and finally the stubborn wires and fuses they tested one at a time, trying to make the turn signals work. I was pulled away from my homework a few times *to learn something important*, like how an alternator works, but really all I learned was how to hand Dad tools and pretend I didn't hear him swearing under his breath.

What's stranger still is that it's after six — nearly dusk. That car should be at the Ritter plant. The shed door squeals on its runners and Dad steps out in his work blues, cradling his favourite gun, a banged-up Winchester .270.

When I was little he would tell me stories about shooting squirrels and rabbits and raccoons, then selling their pelts on the Reserve. Mom's told me since that he was selling them to buy liquor, that he was hunting without a licence, and that he traded an expensive, brand-new and legal .22 for this over-calibred rifle he keeps dead-bolted in the grey steel cabinet in Ralph's shed plus a forty of rye — the bottle that rode shotgun the night he drove out to fight Ralph. She's never said where the rifle was then, but she's never let Dad keep it at home.

Mom shoulders open her door and yells "John!" Dad jumps. It surprises me that the gun doesn't go off. Dad turns to look at her, adjusting his ball cap. Behind his safety glasses his brown eyes grow wide. His mouth forms a straight line, corners edging south in a pre-emptive frown. He's been caught; we know The Look well.

"What are you doing?" Mom calls.

Dad points the muzzle at the ground and steps toward us.

"I'm just doin' Ralph a favour." He uses Grandpa's first name now that they're friends. "I called work," he says. "They know I'm comin' late."

"*John,*" Mom repeats. "*What. Are. You. Doing?*"

I kneel beside Lucy's house and unclasp the chain from her collar. She takes off running, fast for a dog this old, past Dad and toward the bush. He sees me for the first time and abandons The Look.

"Mike," he says. "What are *you* doin' here?"

"Mom asked you first," I say.

Dad shrugs.

"Ralph can't keep the thing." He turns his back to us

and swiftly lifts the rifle. "Same treatment at the pound." I cover my ears and close my eyes as Dad aims into the distance. I wait. No bang. I open again to see Dad's lips muttering as he lowers the gun. He stalks off toward the shed. I take my hands off my ears and listen to him removing the bullets from the rifle and clunking the steel cabinet locked. He stomps outside and launches the sliding door shut, fuming toward the Cutlass. He gets in and slams, growling the muscle car to life, peeling out at the end of the laneway and turning toward Currie. Mom looks at the tire marks on the cement and shakes her head. "Your grandfather will be thrilled with that," she says, and we walk back from the shed to Lucy's doghouse. I take one side, Mom the other, and we lift the creaky structure into the Buick's trunk. As I tie the lid closed fur brushes the backs of my legs. Lucy sniffs me with her dry nose; Ralph had left her water empty, no point in filling it. She jumps on the upholstery when I open the back door. I sit beside her and dodge as she tries to lick my face. Her breath smells like a long-dead fish, dug up from where the pond used to be.

Hyperbolic

*D*EAR PARENT(S)/GUARDIAN(S),

This note is to inform you of your child/ward's introductory session with his/her guidance counsellor. This session is mandatory. Please sign and return the form below confirming your child/ward's appointment time.

M-Z

Mr. D. Rummel
Mrs. L. Kulich

On: **Tuesday, February 15, 1:30pm**
Parent/Guardian signature: *Susan Carrion*

MRS. KULICH HAS TAUGHT math to everyone in Currie Township, most of us for the first time in our Grade Nine homeroom. She's semi-retired now and works in the guidance office, still wearing the red-framed glasses under the increasingly frizzy grey bob, and she teaches just one class, Grade Twelve advanced. She's a good teacher, but I'll never take that course; English is my best mark. This year is my last in compulsory math and then it's on to what I really want to do, which is ... which is what I'm in the guidance office to find out. I wait on a worn tweed couch with wooden arms, and under me every spring feels ready to shoot through the fabric like weeds. The bottom drawer of a dark green file cabinet across the room reads *U.S. Scholarships* and I wonder what it would take to spring-load a basketball in it. I had the same thought last year, waiting for Mr. Brent, who was a real guidance counsellor for twenty-five years before he retired and was replaced by a gym teacher, Mr. Rummel, who's fifty-something and saggily overweight, a cross country coach because Currie High School can't afford football insurance. In a congested voice he calls, "Michael?" and it's still weird. Shouldn't he be healthier? He looks up from my file and studies me as though we've never met. Maybe he just put *C* beside every name. Maybe I didn't care a shit for gym.

"Hi, Coach," I say.

He frowns as he opens his varnished door. "Mr. Rummel will do, now." In his office he flops into the back support on his leather desk chair. I sit on one of the two green-padded steel ones facing him. He discards my file and takes off his glasses, folding them into his shirt pocket with some distress. He looks uncomfortable in anything with buttons. His cheeks droop below the bags under his eyes.

"So—do you know why you're here?" he asks.

"It's mandatory."

He eyes me, scowling a little.

"To talk about my future," I say. "Or something."

"That's right," he says, and there's relief in his exhale.

He doesn't want to be here any more than I do. He picks up my thin record. "Just a check-in," he mumbles, leafing through the paper. "Grades are good ... except for phys. ed."

"No one looks at gym marks."

I've been saving that all week.

"Nah, you're right," he says. He closes the file again and flatly asks, "So what do you want to do with your life?"

I look at the taupe walls and the tack holes Mr. Brent's posters left. The *Star Trek* one was completely ridiculous, but it probably helped the kids he saw most, the kids who got beat up a lot.

"I don't really know," I finally say. "But I want to go to university."

"That's great," Rummel says, smiling. "Just great—but where?"

"I don't know," I say. "I went to a talk in London about Quebec schools. Concordia Journalism looks good."

"Mont-ray-all," he says. "Groovy."

Groovy?

"It's expensive," he says.

"Their tuition's like two-thousand a year *cheaper*."

"Sure. But where are you going to live?"

"A dorm."

"Seven grand a year," he says. "The same no matter where you go."

"Oh."

Were the walls always this close? Was the office always this small?

"So add that to your tuition," he says, taking a pen and a pad of yellow Post-Its from his desk. "Can you count on any help from your parents?"

"My parents?"

"What do they do for a living?"

It's Currie Township. As if he doesn't know.

"My mom works at Vaughan's Bakery," I say. "And my dad's at Ritter Pulley."

He taps the pen on the notepad.

"So how much do they make in a year?"

"I don't know. Mom makes minimum, and Dad's—"

"Well, let's say that you need four-thou for tuition," he says. "More in Ontario, but leave that for a minute. Multiply by four years, that's sixteen. Add seven for your first year, in residence, which makes twenty-three … and your books every year, so twenty-five thousand …"

A lump rises in my throat. I've heard these numbers on game shows, but Rummel is no Alex Trebek.

"… plus you're going to need rent, food and utilities for three more years …"

He scribbles furiously.

"… let's say five more per, so fifteen, which gives us a total of …"

He peels off the Post-It and hands it to me.

I pinch the note and stare at his sums. I don't look up. I won't let him know he's gotten to me.

"I'll live at home and drive to Western," I say slowly. "If I have to. And I have a job." I've worked a year already at Russ Bevan's egg farm — walking distance down the road, and under the table—and I'll be sixteen in the summer. I'm already looking at student factory jobs around London: GM Diesel, Diamond Aircraft, Sterling Trucks. They're almost an hour's drive, but they pay double what anything out here does.

"How much you got in the bank?"

"Some," I mutter.

None of your fucking business.

He smirks and asks, "What were you saving for?" making sure to hang on the auxiliary verb.

"A car."

Rummel laughs. He shakes his head.

"Maybe you don't need the car."

"How will I get to work?"

"You got a bicycle?" he asks.

I stare through him.

"So you want to have a car *and* go to university?" He laughs again. "When did you strike it rich?"

I look at the floor and say nothing.

"And what about expenses? You got any now?"

"No," I say. "Not really." I can't admit to still buying hockey cards, or the if-he-gets-to-fifty-bucks-he'll-do-it collections taken up in the caf to get some twelfth-grader to jump into the Waubnakee River after school, or the thirty bucks my friends and I take turns overpaying [name withheld] for the beer we drink on weekends at [name also withheld]'s place. Rummel pulls his chair closer to me and looks over his puffy cheeks and a nose I now realize is too red. I can smell it on him. He's drunk.

"That's good," he says, "but you need more money. What are you going to do?"

I grit my teeth and try to look out a window. There aren't any. I look back and his eyes pin me to the chair.

"You said my marks are good. I could go for scholarships."

He fans the pages in my folder and scoffs.

"They'd have to be *very* good."

"What about student loans?"

"They're a rip-off. The interest makes you poorer in the long run."

Is he serious?

He leans in. He is.

"So," he says. "What makes you think you can go to university?"

I slump in my chair, ducking under his gaze. He's waiting for me to break.

"I work hard," I say. "You don't know. And I'll get another job, and still do all my homework, and I never skip class, and—"

"You know what I think?" he says. "I think you should join the army."

I close my eyes and lower my head.

"It's the only way you can afford it," he says. He stands and steps out from behind the desk, coming around to sit in the other chair, beside me. The girls I know say he's a creep; the guys don't say anything. He puts his hand on my shoulder and says, "Trust me."

I brush it off, spitting a "Don't touch me" as I stand up.

He switches back to his smile.

"Okay, champ—back to class. Glad we had this little talk."

He holds his door open and I walk through, scuffling

past Mrs. Kulich and the frosted glass windows to the hall. I head straight for the boys' room, which is empty when I step in. I lock a stall door behind me and I sit atop the toilet tank, resting my feet on the black seat. I scream from the bottom of my chest and I drop my head into my hands. I sniffle. I wipe my eyes and notice a scribbled conversation on the wall.

In rusty orange there are more words, engraved in the yellow paint above the toilet roll.

CURRIE HIGH SCHOOL GRADUATION DIPLOMAS
⬇

This author must have stolen a punch set from metal shop. I take some paper and blow my nose before leaving the stall, then I stare into the mirror until I've promised myself I'll never tell anyone what just happened.

I LAST UNTIL dinner at our hand-me-down table.
"Mike, don't you want more potatoes?" Mom asks.
"No, thanks," I say. "I'm not very hungry."

"I don't believe you," Mom says. "We're already through two bags of milk this week. You're growing. You're *always* hungry."

"I had a big lunch."

"That's never stopped you before," Dad says. "What's the matter? Some girl think she's too good for you?"

"That's not—"

"She's not so great," he says. "She still shits brown."

"Dad, that's not it!"

"John, really?" Mom says, frowning. "Language." Nancy giggles. Mom turns to her and says, "Eat your dinner." Nancy resumes forking potatoes.

"Oh," Mom says, and it flashes in her eyes. She remembers. "How was your guidance appointment?"

"Fine," I mumble.

Shit.

"Really?"

I shake my head. My lip quivers.

"What?" Mom asks. She looks helplessly at Dad. He shrugs his shoulders. Nancy doesn't look up from her plate.

"Mr. Rummel—" I say, but then I start to cry.

"Rummel?" Dad says. "Rummel? He's a guidance counsellor now?" He scoops in another mouthful of potatoes and grunts. "That stupid old drunk couldn't guide his arms through his shirtsleeves." We wait while he chews silently, watching his scowl deepen. "How do teachers get to be guidance counsellors, anyway? Does the principal just pick one and say, 'It's your turn now'?"

I don't reply.

"You're letting *that* asshole get to you?" he says, raising his voice. "I thought we taught you better than that." He clatters his fork down on his plate.

"John," Mom says.

"Don't say it, Susan," Dad snaps. "Don't fucking say it. Don't coddle the boy."

Mom breathes out a defeated, "Stop swearing at my table."

He rises from his chair and gathers up his plate. "I'll eat at a different goddamn table, then," he says, making his way down the hall toward the door to the garage.

I look down at my plate and a tear falls in my last bite of potatoes.

Mom asks, "What happened?"

I raise my head and see Nancy's blue eyes off her plate, awaiting my answer. She's scared and still too young to really know we're poor. I blurt, "Can I be excused?" and I don't wait for an answer. In the mudroom I throw my coat over my shoulders and plant my feet in my boots without tying them. The door of our house slams behind me — the only house east of the tracks in Waubnakee. The town had grown with the railroad until sometime in the thirties, and on our acre lot was once the Reese Hotel, where rail workers lodged between shifts. The librarian at school says other people stayed nights, too: people just passing through, who got off the train to see the town.

Tourists.

Here.

But the black-and-white *Waubnakee Seed* photos in the school's microfiche prove it, chronicling guests up to the last three, the masked men who lit the Reese Hotel Fire. Articles alongside say the Reese had been a bootlegging front and a score had been settled. The hotel had been the first sign of an east side of town, but after the fire nothing was built beyond the tracks until sometime in the sixties, when our house finally replaced the burned-out ruin.

Waubnakee has since shrunk to two hundred people, and most of them floor their gas pedals at the stop sign and charge up County Road 17 — Main Street — then vault the level crossing and rocket out of town, launching empty beer bottles onto our lawn as they do.

Past the tracks I wander the town's seven other streets for an hour, until my treads clog with wet snow and my every step teeters.

WHEN I GET home, Nancy is in bed and Mom and Dad are winding down; Mom has tomorrow off, but Dad will be up at five for work. When I come in the door they meet me, and Mom warms the kettle for tea, a small peace. I tell them about the meeting and they listen on the couch. I don't know how Mom talked Dad into sitting through this. His eyes keep closing, and Mom keeps swatting his shoulder, softly at first and then hard enough to bruise. He sits up with a sharp shout.

At the story's end, Mom asks, "So what did you do?"

"Nothing," I say. I hang my head. "I didn't do a damned thing."

She sighs.

"Language," she says.

IN THE MORNING Mom calls the school from the kitchen. She motions to me to pick up her bedroom extension, and when I get there and put it to my ear she's on hold. I turn the mouthpiece up away from my lips and cover it with my hand before the principal, Mr. Johanssen, answers "Hello," exasperated like it's already his last call of the day.

"My son saw Mr. Rummel yesterday — the *so-called* guidance counsellor," Mom says. "Tell me: how, *exactly*, did a gym teacher end up doing this job?"

Mr. Johanssen sighs. "Mr. Rummel is qualified," he says without emotion. "What's your concern, I'll discuss it with him."

"Oh, no," Mom replies. "You put him on the phone this instant. *I* will discuss this with him."

"You want to do my job?" he says. "Fine with me."

The line goes dead, and after two hold beeps we hear the stuffy voice.

"Coach Rummel — I mean, Art Rummel speaking — I mean, hello, this is Mr. Rummel?"

"How dare you," Mom says, not bothering to explain.

"I'm sorry?"

"How dare you talk to my son like that!"

"Who is this?" he asks.

"It's Susan Carrion. You saw my son yesterday."

Silence.

"And who's your son?"

"Michael! God, you don't even know *which* lives you're ruining! My son is Michael Carrion, you idiot!"

"And when did I see him? Yesterday?"

"Yes! You saw him yesterday! You harangued him about money, and you told him he should run off and join the army! Ring a bell?"

I haven't heard Mom shout like this ... well, ever.

"Oh, yeah," Rummel says. "Standard Grade Ten Boy Speech. Exaggerate to scare the hell out of the kid — makes him go through with whatever he plans to do, just so he can come home and rub it in my face one day." He wheezes and mutters, "Not like that's worth coming home for, though. Stupid kids."

"Stupid kids?" Mom yells. "Stupid kids? This is a school! You could fix that! But no, you'd just rather — "

"If they're not so stupid," Rummel says, "they'll figure it out."

Mom lowers her voice to an ice-cold register and asks, "Where do you get off?"

"Listen, Mrs." — he clears his throat — "whatever your name is."

"Carrion! My name is Susan Carrion!"

He thinks a minute.

"Carrion ... John's wife? Susan ... Burford?"

"Yes," Mom says.

"You had a sister ... Beautiful girl ..."

"I still do." She snorts. "She just doesn't live here anymore. Imagine."

"Mm-hmm," Rummel says. "Listen, Susan. I retrained for this job because no one else would, and the school couldn't afford someone specialized. It was this or forced retirement. You can tell these kids they can be astronauts if you want, but they have to transfer out of district for *introductory* physics. What am I supposed to do?"

Mom doesn't answer.

"Currie hasn't changed," he says in a softer voice. "I push the good kids out any way I can."

"But did you have to suggest *the army!?*" Mom asks. While she waits for an answer I set the phone gently on the bed. I cross the hall to my room to gather today's books, English and math, hyperbole and hyperbolae, knowing full well Rummel's already hung up.

Mercy

IN WAUBNAKEE, WE don't have a pitcher's mound. The base paths aren't lined, and the infield's not grass, and the superintendent drives the county truck out from Currie just once a spring to drag the gravel flat. You'd think he cuts the outfield just as often. We like the Jays fine, but on summer nights we live for softballs wheeled underhand, rising as they travel the forty feet from pitcher to batter, and the aluminum ping of long drives over four-man outfields, displacing the humidity and the whirring mosquitoes while in a tank-top and jean cut-offs in the canteen Jessie Mueller roasts hotdogs and pouts, "What can I do *you* for?"

Mothers in Waubnakee use her as the example. In our yard yesterday, my own bawled out my sister for hanging shirts on the clothesline by the shoulders. "It stretches out the neck!" she yelled from the back door. "You think Jessie Mueller's got it bad? Just you *try* dressing like that, missy, tits hanging out for the whole town to see. *I* won't pick you up at the police station."

It's a natural leap for Mom, and it has been since she got into Ray Tarkington's Mustang on a Friday in August, 1978. Ray's father drove that car to London two months later and pushed his son out at Wolesley Barracks; from there the army shipped him to Gagetown, New Brunswick. I was born the next spring, on a Sunday, just before the Men's League game. Mom says the Wanderers missed Ray that year, and finished last in the county. He came home on leave when I was two and married Mom, but when she got pregnant with Nancy he left again, for good, via telephone. John Carrion, once the classmate from down the road who Mom had helped with his math homework at Mrs. Kulich's discreet request, moved in before Nancy was born, when he and Mom were both twenty. We know now he's not our father but Nancy and I still call John "Dad." He's done more for us than Ray ever did.

As clean-up hitter, Ray's replacement was Jessie's bearded, beer-bellied father, Hank. "Your old boy could hit the ball a mile," he told me once, in front of Dad, of course, staring at him and challenging him. "I even seen him put it *on the road* one time," he said, which *is* pretty far—provided that it actually happened. But if anyone would know, it was Hammerin' Hank, who got the nickname like Greenberg and Aaron for his bat, plus the one time he chased a boyfriend of Jessie's off his property with a twelve-pound sledge. We look over our shoulders before we say it.

Hank drives tow truck for a living, and four springs ago he bought Dad's beloved blue Chev after dragging it home from Highway 401. The pickup needed a three-dollar valve, not a new motor like he'd said, and was back on the road in a month. And a year after that, during Grade Eight graduation while I was being handed the

English Award for my journal entry about that very truck, Jessie was sneaking out the back door of the gym with the spare key she had swiped from her mom's purse, to drive to a high school bush party. Hank charged her with theft, and when the case finally went to court she got community service. That's why she makes hotdogs now.

JESSIE AND I have sisters the same age, too, thirteen. Hers are twins, Rebecca and Stacey, and they're tall and athletic and already assured a spot on *senior* volleyball when they start at Currie High School this fall; Nancy, on the other hand, played one season of soccer in Currie when she was seven, and after three games it ended with a goal post and a broken tooth. Now she likes to read books about flying insects and she wanders around our backyard identifying them — but this morning Mom signed her up for fastball anyway. The registration table is set up every year on the warning track in front of the chain link, black tile-topped outfield fence, and beyond that there's a plaque on the shed-sized Currie Township Museum that says Waubnakee's been here two-hundred years. Nancy's will be the first girls' team anyone remembers — and though population records show that there have always been enough girls eleven to thirteen to field a squad, all around the one-room museum where the walls join the ceiling, photos of Waubnakee's most accomplished women cast judgment through bright tacky eye shadow. Fall Fair Princesses give way to Homemaking Queens, who keep watch over the *pièce de resistance*, the Waubnakee Recipe Archive.

So are teenage girls in Waubnakee suddenly into fastball? Not remotely. There's one legit job in town, at Pete Quinn's ValuGas, evenings, five-to-ten; Dad had it when he was in high school, and now I've got it. Everyone else works down the highway in London, or at least as far as Currie, and no one's parents get home before seven.

A month ago, the Mueller twins deliberately missed the bus from Currie Elementary to ride home in a twelfth-grader's Camaro. He was lucky to drop them off while Hank was on a call. When word got out, parents said, "Boys will be boys," but they must have called a meeting and they must have chosen fastball.

What scares them most is girls being girls.

I QUIT PLAYING ball when I started working for Pete, and most nights I watch the Blue Jays on the little rabbit-eared TV beside the till. We lock the pumps when the Wanderers play, on Tuesday nights and long weekend Sundays, and we tape a battered note to the door that says AT THE BALL PARK. COME GET US IF YOU NEED GAS.

We've never missed a pitch.

Tonight, a Friday, I show up early and ask Pete, "Do you mind staying?" I've played catch with Nancy in our yard all week, in the hour between school and work, and her first practice is about to start. "I promised my sister I'd come watch," I say. "She's afraid everyone will laugh at her."

Pete tucks his grey hair behind his ears, under his green Seedcorp mesh-back, and he chuckles. He bends to open the cabinet below the register and I hear him tear off new tape. He produces the note and says, "I'll come, too." We follow the gravel lane behind the gas bar to the park, where ten girls sulk on the bleachers in bad pre-teen makeup. Tonight's also the monthly youth dance in Currie — no coincidence — and rides to Centennial Arena's upstairs lounge hinge on going to practice.

From the group of parents milling around the canteen, tanned, smiley Shawn Baylor emerges. He's just over thirty, and he moved here this winter from London, where both of his daughters played. He introduces himself as the coach and leads the girls onto the field. They drag their feet until he sits them on the grass in a half-circle. His oldest, Christine, will be pitcher, he says, and her sister, Samantha — who's only ten — will catch. The rest of the girls sigh in relief. It's short-lived.

"Who wants to play first base?" Shawn asks.

No one volunteers.

He frowns.

"Second?"

Silence.

"How about third?"

No response.

"Well, then," he says. "You must all be shortstops."

"What's a shortstop?" Nancy asks.

Shawn leans in to close the sale. "It's the best position, between second and third." He smiles. "You'll get a lot of balls hit to you."

"Then no," Nancy says, shaking her head.

"We should put our best athlete there, anyway," he says. "Rebecca. And our other best athlete" — he gestures to Stacey—"in centre field." He assigns the other positions seemingly at random, though Nancy in right field can't be an accident.

The girls partner off along the first-base line and play catch to warm up. Shawn walks from pair to pair and takes one player aside at a time, to demonstrate throws from the shoulder, not the elbow or wrist. When he calls away a freckle-faced farm girl named Melissa—Nancy's partner—my sister stands still and looks at the ground, too shy to ask another pair if she can join. She brought my dusty old equipment bag, which sits on the bench now. I walk to the cage and take out my glove; the worn leather embraces my fingers like old friends as I jog onto the field. Nancy throws the ball to me and we play like we did in the yard: she dodges my soft tosses and her hardest land well in front of me. Melissa returns, and I throw with her while Shawn talks to Nancy. He continues down the line, and so do I, until he's talked to the last player. He wolf-whistles and sends the girls to their positions. I take off my glove and start toward the bleachers. Shawn calls, "Mike! Mind hitting a few?" I shrug and turn back for a bat. While I splash softballs everywhere but right field—I never could go the other way—Shawn moves around the diamond, talking to each fielder about her role. He becomes the pitcher afterward, and I replace each girl who's in for batting practice, offering the odd tip to my neighbours in the field. They uniformly roll their eyes. The last batter finishes and Shawn ends the practice. The girls all sprint for the parking lot. I walk to the bench and hand Shawn the bat.

"Think you could come back next week?" he asks.

All the parents may be in on the plan, but apparently, Shawn's the only coach. Before I answer, engines rumbling to life startle me. I look toward the parking lot, past right field, and past the canteen, where Jessie's lowering the window flap, standing on tiptoes to unlock it for the boys' game, up next. Her long black ponytail brushes her pale shoulders, bare except for two light purple slivers, the straps of her tank-top.

I look to Pete for permission, who's caught me staring. He laughs and winks. "The note'll cover you," he says.

WE EXPECT TO lose when we arrive in Currie the next Friday. They have twenty times Waubnakee's population — enough for a Blue team and a White team, even in girls' league — and because only one of them can be the champion, the association gives Blue to the longest-tenured coach, who stacks it. This is the team waiting on the diamond, warming up in blue jackets, blue jersey numbers sewn on white sleeves.

Our girls choose yellow, white-screened *Waubnakee* tees from a cardboard box in Shawn's minivan moments before the game. When they take the field for the top of the first, Shawn tells me he thought about pink, but that he knew some of the mothers would object. He laughs.

"The goal is to get their minds *off* being pretty," he says.

Blue scores the eight-run limit with ease, and in our half, our batters strike out, one-two-three. In the second, Blue tacks on another seven, putting the score to 15–0. Bill McLaren, the sixty-year-old umpire, signals to both coaches. The game is over.

"Mercy rule," Shawn mutters. He looks at his watch. "Twenty minutes." The parents in the bleachers start grousing about gas money. Shawn waves Blue's coach over and, after a short discussion, Waubnakee takes on Blue's back-up pitcher and half their hitters. We send back our neediest and hope they'll soak up some skill as we play out the time slot. In the last inning of the new game, when "Waubnakee" is only down 4–0, Rebecca screams a triple past first base. From third she calls to the next batter, Nancy, "Come on! Hit me home!"

In the bigs, the call would be the squeeze: a bunt toward first to disorient the fielders while the runner on third races home. The Braves tried it in '92 against the Jays, for the Series, but Timlin threw to Carter in time. Nancy puts a full swing on the first pitch and accomplishes the same, a dribbler between the pitcher and first. At the sound of the ping, Rebecca leaves third, and with a head-first slide more like a belly flop she scores. The pitcher stands, ball in hand, watching the play at home, and she turns around too late to throw Nancy out at one. Our girls scream — even the ones fielding for "Blue" — and they run to the plate to surround Rebecca, our new captain, who rises wincing from the swirling grey dust.

BUSINESS PICKS UP at ValuGas the last week of July, when Ritter closes for maintenance and its workers take their families to Lake Erie. I used to go, too, but now I'm needed close to home to fill cars and get everyone else out of here. Mom and Dad left tonight for New Highlands, a park in a little beach town called Scotsport where

Grandpa Ralph keeps a trailer he never uses, and they took Nancy with them, still in her uniform after Waubnakee's first win, 4–3 over the team from the Reserve. As the Buick pulled away from the diamond, Mom joked "No big parties!" through the window, but she knew I'd have a few friends over for a bonfire. I invited ten, but with most people gone to the lake, the only one I'm betting on is Brian Callaghan. I told him to come around eight, so when I walk across the tracks at seven-thirty, his Dad's maroon rust-bucket van is already in the yard, doors open, its factory-issue speakers farting out the classic rock station. Brian sits on a red cooler as I approach, unfolding a black fibreglass tent pole, and when I turn down my laneway he's just blond-frosted buzz-cut and broad shoulders, kneeling on the six-man canvas on the ground. Over *Light my Fire* I yell, "Brian!" I hate The Doors. This station seems to play them every fifteen minutes.

"Just in time," Brian says without looking up. He pushes the pole through its sleeve, the last one, and he motions across the tent. "Grab the other side?"

"I told you, everyone's gone," I say. "There's room in the house." But I walk around the tent anyway and bend down to grasp the fabric. I take one sleeve in each hand and support the tent while he circles it. The poles arc as he secures them in the eyelets. He walks the few feet from the tent to its bag and he pulls out the fly.

"I put clean sheets on Nancy's bed for you," I say.

Brian laughs and throws the fabric over the tent.

"Be a man," he says. "It's a beautiful night." He walks the circle again, hooking each stretchy cord into its ring. "No wind. No need to peg it."

We each lift a side of the cooler and carry it to the back of the lot beside the fire pit, a rusty truck rim in a hole in the ground. I take some kindling from the rotting cardboard box beside the woodpile against the wire fence that separates our yard from the cornfield and I pile it in the centre of the pit. I light it. Mom and Dad sit out here practically every night, and they've left two lawn chairs folded out. I sit down in one and Brian hands me a beer. His chair creaks and wobbles as he sits down, too. He clinks his bottle to mine and we drink.

"How's ball?" he asks.

"The girls got their first win tonight," I say.

Brian laughs.

"I meant your team."

"I told you, I'm working this summer. I need the money."

"Pete closes Tuesdays," he says. "Why aren't you playing Men's League?"

I take a long drink from the bottle.

"I'm not good enough, Brian."

"So what? I mean, you'd never have made Blue, but you could always slap singles. And you're a good right fielder."

"A slap-hitting right fielder. Just what every team wants." I laugh. "A good right fielder is a bad ballplayer. It's where you bury home run hitters, just to keep them in the batting order."

Now it's Brian who takes a long pull. He was never much of a pitcher, and he shot up eight inches this school year. He's still on Blue's bench, but now he can't hit the broadside of a barn.

"I play right field."

"Yeah," I say, "and you hit home runs."

He laughs.

"Once in a while."

I get up and walk to the woodpile again, where I choose a big block. It kicks up a few sparks from the old coals, reignited from last night and the night before that. I stand and watch a moment, thinking, "It can be so peaceful out here," when Brian says, "Look." Turning into the laneway is a boxy, brown K-Car I recognize from Currie High School's student parking lot. The engine quiets down and Brian follows me around the side of the house. A door clatters shut as we turn the corner and meet his older sister, Stella. She brushes her blonde bangs from her eyes and adjusts an oversized white purse on her shoulder.

"What are you doing here?" Brian asks.

"Just out for a drive," she says, grimacing and motioning to the passenger side where Jessie sits with one hand covering most of her face, her fingertips disappearing into her straight black hair. The bit of cheek we can see is pink, and the corner of a Ziploc bag of ice sticks out, squeezed in her fist.

"Shit," I say.

"Yeah," Stella says.

Brian walks to the car and taps the window, startling Jessie. She turns her head and bends toward the console, shielding her face.

"You okay?" Brian asks. "Come on out."

"Leave her alone," Stella says.

I look over my shoulder when I hear another vehicle, accelerating toward the tracks. It's not Hank's pickup, like I expect, just a small sport truck with no muffler. It roars by.

"He's going to come looking for her," I say.

"At our house," Stella says, glancing at Brian. "He'll never find us here."

"The car's on my front lawn. He'll fucking murder me!"

"So we'll move it," she says. "To the backyard. Close to the house."

"And leave wheel marks? No way! My parents —"

Stella laughs. "Your parents *might* kill you," she says. "Hank *will*." She walks back to the car, not waiting for an answer, and she gets in and starts it. She turns onto the lawn, rounding the house and parking parallel to it with the driver's side wheels nearly in Mom's flowerbeds, so close that after Jessie gets out the passenger side, still holding the ice to her eye, Stella has to follow. She straddles the gearshift, worming her way over the seat.

Jessie takes a few steps away from the car, covering her face with both hands. She exhales and lets her hands fall to her sides. The pink was nothing compared to the purple that's darkening below her eye. "Fuck it," she says, narrowing her gaze at me. "I know I look good with a shiner." It suits her and her dingy red flip flops, toenails unpainted, bare legs under blue jean cut-offs and — no one's perfect — a faded black Doors T-shirt she's cut the neck out of. It sits off her shoulders and unabashedly shows a white strap. Her hair is down. In her hand is a tiny red purse, barely bigger than the pack of cigarettes she pulls from it. She plucks one and puts it between her over-sticked lips, red, too. She lights up.

"Do you want to talk about it?" I ask.

"No," she says.

She bends over and opens the cooler. Bottles clink and ice rumbles. She stands up with her smoke pinched in her mouth, two beers in one hand as the other twists the caps, flicks them to the ground. She gives one bottle to Stella then lifts a hand to her mouth, lowering the cigarette to swig from the beer. Her hands finally come to rest at her sides again.

It is a good look for her.

BRIAN'S ARM IS across my chest when his watch alarm starts beeping. I'm soaked in sweat, and I didn't even sleep *in* the bag, just on it. We unzipped all the windows before passing out, but two guys and fourteen beers do this to a tent. It reeks. With my head pounding, I lift his wrist and crawl to the door. I open the flap and squirm out then walk barefoot on the grass toward the house. I open the screen door gently to temper its squeal, remembering that Jessie and Stella disappeared into the house after just one drink and might still be asleep. But as I enter through the laundry room I hear the shower running. I turn into the kitchen. Stella sits at the table flipping pages in a magazine.

"I got her a towel," she says. "A yellow one. From the hall closet. Is that okay?"

"It's fine."

She doesn't look up from the magazine.

"We'll go once she's out."

"Go where?" I ask.

"Hank's leaving with the twins this morning, for the Lake." She glances side-to-side, as though we're being watched. "We'll have breakfast at Don's to wait him out, then I'll drop Jessie off."

"Hank's leaving her home alone?"

Stella rolls her eyes.

"It was supposed to be a trust exercise ... but yeah."

The judge had also ordered counselling.

"But it was him who hit her, right?" I ask.

Stella nods.

"Why?"

She shakes her head.

"You wouldn't believe me, and I can't tell you anyway." She fumbles in her purse for her car keys. "You guys hungry?" she asks. "I'll drive you back after."

From the bathroom, the shower sound stops. In my mind I see Jessie take the towel from the rack. She dries her feet first and steps over the tub's edge now, wrapping the towel under her armpits, lifting out the wet hair that gets squeezed against her shoulders and letting it fall. Yellow's not her colour. She should take the towel off again.

"Mike?" Stella asks.

"Yeah," I say, back to reality. "Sounds good."

DON'S BREAKFAST IS full of farmers — *retired* farmers — like it is every Saturday. They've eaten here every weekend of their adult lives, at the same tables every time, gawking at generations of young people. When we sit down to fat and salt plates to flush the night before away, people whisper about our mismatched socks (Brian), our messy hair (me), or our wrinkled clothes (Jessie, who clearly slept in the T-shirt). Stella's the only one who looks half-decent, having packed before she left home. We feel the stares as we walk to a booth at the back, though it could be worse: most times, we wait on display in the vestibule. About all Don can cook is a fried egg sandwich, but on Saturdays the line-up's out the door regardless.

Brian and I each get the Strapping Lad, three of everything: eggs, sausages, bacon and ham slices, with toast and homefries on the side. Stella gets the sandwich and Jessie gets nothing, just a coffee when grouchy old Marlene says: "Something to drink, at least?" before she and her change pouch jingle off and leave our table in silence, the kind that would go unnoticed most hangover mornings but looms like a funnel cloud across from Jessie and her still-puffy eye. The coffee arrives, and then our plates. Jessie watches us devour our meals. I convince her to have a slice of my toast. She turns down the jam. When we finish our food Brian and I stare at Jessie. Stella stares at us. The farmers are still staring at our table. Jessie glances at each of us in turn.

"Done?" she asks.

We look to each other, to agree that we are, but before we answer Jessie has pushed herself up with her hands and brought her feet onto the bench. She stands and steps onto the table and screams: *"I had an abortion, and my father hit me for it!"*

Forks clatter down on plates. Conversations end. Jessie jumps down, kind of whimpers and runs to the front door and out. Stella and I each throw a twenty on the table, way more than the bill will come to; we forget the change and hurry after, finding Jessie in Stella's passenger seat. We join her in the car and leave Currie, down the Sixth Concession toward Waubnakee.

When we're out of town, I lean forward and ask: "Who told him?"

Jessie sighs, doesn't look back. "Mitchell himself. After ball one night."

Chad Mitchell. Captain and starting catcher for Currie Blue, and a star now in Men's League, the only one that scouts out here. I didn't think he and Jessie were together, but I guess they are. Or were. I hope it's were.

Jessie turns and looks out her window. She exhales.

"Hank and I were doing so well, too."

In the cluttered yard in front of the Muellers' leaning, mint-coloured house, we don't see the baby-blue truck. Stella pulls the car off just past the long laneway, to back in. She keeps it running. When Jessie gets out she leaves her door open. We wait in silence as she enters the house, holding our breath till she emerges again. She flashes a thumbs-up. No Hank, no speeding escape. No chase down gravel roads.

THE MEN'S TEAM is in first place going into the playoffs. The final game is Labour Day Sunday, like always, but it's at night, pushed back by the girls' year-end tournament, which rotates between Currie and Somewhere Else; as the new team this year, Waubnakee is Somewhere Else.

The girls' last regular season game was their best, a 2–1 loss to Blue. The twins have played even better since Hank began coaching, as of the first game after Lake Week. He yells a lot—"*Rebecca! Two hands!*" or "*Dammit, Stacey! Choke up!*"—but it's working for them. And though the other girls haven't improved much, a shortstop, a centre-fielder and decent pitching can really carry a team: we finished a distant second to Blue, one win ahead of White.

I get to the diamond early, to unlock the equipment shed behind the backstop so Bill the umpire can start spiking the bases down. Hank's already on the field when I arrive, wearing his Wanderers jersey and leading the twins in furious jumping jacks. I sit on the bleachers and watch. Shawn's van drives up and Christine and Samantha jump out the side door. They jog to the field. Shawn shakes his head as he approaches, rolled up bat rack in hand. His eyes dart side-to-side, then he smiles.

"Hammerin' Hank." He shrugs. "What can you do?" He hands me the schedule the league office sent him and I walk it to the snack bar. I take the cover off the chalkboard beside the window and begin posting game times. To my left, a voice, not Jessie's, asks, "Can you give me a hand?" It's her mom, Jane Mueller, who coaches figure skating in Currie and who's been running the canteen for a month now. I hold one corner of the flap as she undoes the padlock. We lower the plywood together.

"Thank you," she says, adjusting her glasses.

I say, "No problem." She lingers a moment, expecting small talk, I think, but I don't say more. I haven't seen Jessie since that morning at Don's, and I haven't asked—I wouldn't dare with Hank so close.

Brian told me, though, after Stella told him: Jessie's a free woman again.

WAUBNAKEE PLAYS THE first game, against the team from the Reserve. I say it that way because everyone else calls them the Reds or the Indians, and the league has decked them out in knock-off Cleveland gear that's even more embarrassing than the mismatched, second-hand ball pants and raglans all their teams wear. Only two adults accompany the girls, one to coach and the other to drive their rusty mini school bus. Our team takes the field for the top of the first and I know that today, we'll do the mercying.

Hank made it a verb in his speech before the game.

"Remember how it felt to get *mercied*?" He gestured to three keeners from Blue in the bleachers, here early enough to see our game. "They know you're comin'," he said. "And we almost *beat* 'em last time." He paused for effect. "Run up the score here. Send a message."

In the bottom of three, the girls walk off the field with the score 15–0 for us. No matter how bad you've got it, someone's always got it worse.

I'M WATCHING OUR second game closely, from the coach's box at third base. We're up 7–5 in the fourth, runner on third, one out, when behind right field, the baby blue pickup pulls in; Hank's on the bench, though. He and the girls came in the Muellers' minivan. The truck door opens and Jessie steps down, slamming it behind her. She walks toward the diamond in a fuchsia golf shirt. What's left of her hair is short and parted to one side, more conservative but more punk rock than before (black eye notwithstanding). Watching her, I don't hear a deep foul ball ping, well over my head and still in play. White's leftfielder races toward the fence and crashes in, catching it. From the bench, Hank hollers, "Tag! Tag!"

The runner, Melissa, looks at me quizzically.

I yell, "Yes! Run! That means run!"

She pushes off and starts toward home, getting to the plate just before the throw without sliding. Most of the girls are still scared to slide. On the back of my neck I feel Hank's laser eyes, but I don't turn to look at the bench.

Jessie's just sat down in the bleachers.

She waves at me, ever so slightly.

IN THE TOP of the last inning, with two out, White scores two runs on a double by a speedy redhead. It closes the gap to 8–7. The next batter steps in and from the bench White's players sing "H-O, H-OM, H-O-M-E, R-U-N" and clap their hands. The batter, short with long brown hair, swings at the first pitch and scuffs it. The ball rolls slowly toward third base, barely past the pitcher. Rebecca charges hard and calls off Christine—"Mine! *Mine*!"— before scooping it and whipping it off-balance to Melissa at first base, beating the runner by half a step and ending the game. Our girls run onto the field and celebrate around the bag, throwing their gloves in the air and cheering. They're through to the final. As they line up at the plate for the handshake, my shoulder is shoved from behind and I stumble. I turn around. Hank stands with his arms folded, hat in his hand, nostrils flaring.

"Get your head in the game, *Carrion*," he says, poking my chest. "Your real dad would be so disappointed. We nearly didn't score that. What the hell were you thinking?"

"I don't know," I say. "I'm sorry."

"These girls have to *win*," he says. He wipes his forehead with the back of his hand. "You understand?"

I nod.

"What?" he barks.

"Yes," I say, straightening my spine and lifting my head, which is finally enough for him. He replaces his cap and stalks off toward Shawn. They talk in low tones then head for Shawn's van. I walk to the bleachers and sit beside Jessie. Around us, Blue's players are rising from their seats, gathering their equipment. We stay silent as Blue takes the field and one of their girls starts batting grounders to a few teammates on the base paths. Our players have begun walking toward the parking lot, where they'll get into parents' vehicles and ride to Shawn's place for barbecued hamburgers before the final. Passing them the other way is the Reserve team, leaving the rusty bus for a last, meaningless game. I watch absently as they sleepwalk toward the diamond.

Jessie exhales heavily.

"What?" I ask.

She turns to me, then looks away again.

"No," she says. "It's too corny."

"Come on. What?" I ask again.

"Well," she says, "it's just … this has been really good for Rebecca and Stacey … and for the other girls, too. I mean, something to throw themselves into, and …"

"And what?"

"And it makes me wonder if things could have been different for me."

She leans forward to pick a few blades of grass and tosses them up, letting the breeze take them.

"Hank always wanted me to play, too," she says. "On the boys' team."

I imagine her sliding in a dust cloud at second base — cleats up — with a black stripe under each eye. She stands and dusts herself off, nodding back at me first base. (I moved her over, hustling out the bunt.)

She's waiting for me to say something.

"Why didn't you?" I ask.

She looks in my eyes an extra long moment.

"I'll skate for Mom," she says, "but I fucking *hate* softball."

I reach over and take her hand. She doesn't flinch but she says, "Not here." She rises from her seat. I stand and follow her along the first-base fence to Hank's pickup. My pickup. Jessie takes a crowded ring of keys from her purse. She puts one in my door.

"He left you the truck?"

"His ball equipment, too," she says, smiling, unlocking it.

"Trust exercise?"

"It is now," she says.

I pull my door shut as she gets behind the wheel. She starts the engine and reaches for Hank's Rothmans on the dashboard, putting one in her mouth and offering me the pack. I've been trying not to smoke but I take one, which she lights for me. I breathe in and cough. She cracks the window and shifts the truck into drive. We turn off the park laneway at the museum, onto Waubnakee's one backstreet, and then we accelerate onto Seventeen. We vault the tracks in front of my house. Jessie keeps the pedal depressed. My knuckles go white around the armrest on the door.

"Relax," she says. "I have my licence."

Same grade but a year older, I remember.

"Where are we going?" I ask. She doesn't answer or even glance away from the windshield.

"What happened to you, Jessie? Where have you been?"

She pulls the last drag off her cigarette and throws it out the window. She finally takes her eyes off the road.

"Don't laugh," she says.

"I won't."

"Bible Camp." I keep my promise and let Jessie break first. Her laugh is loud, too loud, and it scares me. It sounds hungry. "The day after I saw you, when my parents came home … they drove me there. Four weeks. I got back yesterday."

"And Mitchell?" I ask.

She turns to me again, eyes wide, mad.

"What about him?"

"Did you two talk about—"

"No," she says. "Not really. He's moving to Sarnia. He thinks he broke up with me, but …"

"But?"

"We haven't talked," she says. "Not since he drove me London to—" She pauses. "The baby."

We near the dirt road along the Waubnakee River —the cleverly named River Road—and turn onto it, following it until it can't help but cross, just outside of

Currie. Jessie stops the truck on the clattering steel bridge, so close to the barrier that she nearly scrapes it, trapping me inside the cab. If I want out, I'll have to go through her, but she leads, opening her door and jumping down. I hear the tailgate clang and the truck's old springs groan. Her footsteps echo in the chassis. I open the back window to talk to her, but when I see her I know she won't answer. She stands staring down at Hank's equipment bag. A frog croaks. Suddenly—violently—Jessie bends and lifts the bag by its straps, swaying a moment before she screams, low and throaty, "*I hate you!*" and throws it over the railing. She loses her balance and thuds on the truck floor. The bats and balls clunk on the rocks. The river's nearly dry this late in summer.

"He's going to kill you," I say.

Jessie shakes her head.

"Everyone knows, now," she says. She sniffs. "All he can do is send me away again."

She lifts one foot over the side of the box, and using the tire as a foothold she jumps down.

"Is that what you want?"

As though she doesn't hear, Jessie walks to her still-open door. She lifts off her shirt and throws it in at me as she steps up from the running board, crawls over my legs. She reaches for my fly. The sun's in my eyes the whole time, and afterward we listen to the shallow water below us burble softly, like it's washing us clean.

JESSIE LETS ME out at the end of the park lane, on her way home to pack what she can. A few Waubnakee parents are already parked in the lot so we don't kiss goodbye. I make up something to tell Shawn about where I've been, but when I get to the bench he doesn't ask.

After warm-up, Hank herds the girls into the cage. He stands in the doorway and talks of trophies and execution. Shawn and I flank him and add nothing.

"And last thing," Hank says. "Nobody—I mean *nobody* —swings at the first pitch. If you do, you sit the next inning. It's discipline. Make her throw you strikes."

Blue's the top seed, so they're the home team. Their pitcher comes out tired in the top of the first, starting her third game today. She throws twelve straight balls, which loads the bases. Rebecca steps in next and clears them with a triple: second pitch, a fast one, way outside. She calls, "Come on, Stace," as her sister picks up a bat. The first pitch to Stacey comes in slower than it should, straight down the pipe, and she swings and powers the ball over the outfielders. It booms off the black tile atop the fence, inches from where Hank usually puts it, and the ball caroms back past the centre fielder, who chases in vain. The easy home run is Stacey's first, it makes the score 5–0, and if the plaque-'n'-shack museum would make some room it would be enshrined as the Girls' League distance record, too. At the plate, Rebecca waits and slaps her sister high-ten. The grinning twins return to the bench, where the team has lined up to greet them. Hank waits behind the fence and glares. Stacey meets his eyes. Her smile disintegrates. She slumps and drags her feet as she walks off the field, arms lowered, ignoring the raised hands greeting her. The girls stand aside and let Stacey shuffle down the bench in silence. The whole team turns and stares at scowling Hank, who ignores them and looks at his clipboard.

He calls the next name: Nancy. We've made her bunt a lot this season — it's the only way to get her on base, and the twins ahead of her are fast enough they can usually move over. She looks at me and waits for the usual sign, but I don't tap my belt buckle. We exchange a glance.

Fuck him. Swing away.

The first pitch is good and Nancy rips past it wildly. She cuts again at the second, a mile outside, grinning as she does. She connects on the third, in on her wrists, and lamely pops the ball up to the catcher. As usual, the bench greets her with half-hearted "Good try" and "You'll get her next time," which we taught the girls to say after a bad out, when there's nothing to say at all. Nancy takes her seat at the end of the bench, beside Stacey.

Melissa hits next, and she doesn't even look at me. She swings through three straight, and so does Samantha. Blue hustles off. Six of our girls retrieve their gloves and take the field. The other four stay glued to the bench.

Melissa's green eyes gleam.

"You can't sit us all," she says, taunting Hank.

Bill the umpire calls, "Hurry up, yellow team!" Hank grunts and sends everyone but Stacey out, playing one short to make his point. In his haste, he sends Nancy to centre field, and as if they're aiming at her — which they well might be — Blue's players pound ball after ball over her head. Eight runs come in, the limit for the inning, and after Waubnakee goes down in order in the top of the second — three more swinging strikeouts — Blue scores the maximum again. We get nothing in the top of three:

long fly out for Rebecca, strikeout for Stacey, and a pop-up to the pitcher by Nancy. Blue scores a quick four runs in the bottom.

20–5.

Bill waves a hand at Hank.

"Mercy rule," he announces. "Game's over."

Blue cheers and rushes from their bench. Hank leaps off ours and kicks the bat rack off the fence. He throws everything he can find onto the field: batting helmets, spare gloves, the scorebook, more, and he stomps toward the parking lot. Shawn and I line our girls up for the handshake. Blue gets the trophy, and afterward, the Waubnakee parents greet their daughters in the bleachers, where they put hands on shoulders and sigh and walk together to their cars.

Nancy helps me retrieve the team gear from the field, and at the shed we find Shawn unlocking it for Bill, who takes a hammer and walks back to the diamond, where he begins moving the bases back for the men's final.

Shawn asks Nancy, "Think you'll be back next year?"

She stares through him and doesn't answer.

"It's all right," he says. "I'm not sure either."

Nancy and I say goodbye to him and we follow the third-base line out of the park. We turn down the backstreet. We cross the tracks. From our lawn we still hear Hank cursing in the parking lot. I picture the twins and Jane in the minivan, rigid in their seats and making sure to not look out the door at him. In his tirade he yells Jessie's name over and over, and I wonder how far she'll get this time.

Young Buck

I KNOW WHY Mike didn't take the shot.

It had been coming all week. It had been coming fifteen years.

Susan and I had raised him on venison hunted five days every November, when a dozen guys turn off the world and take their muskets to Ralph's place, filling the spare rooms and the pull-out couches in the basement. When there were more of us we needed air mattresses on the living room carpet, too. For the most part, the guys are Ralph's age, so complaining about your back hurting from where you slept is part of the fun now. You bitch about the cold, the rain, the mud and all the bushwhacking; how you're too old to walk so far, how your wife said you might think about skipping the deer hunt this year—fat chance, you said—and about the farmer who somehow hasn't taken his corn off yet, how it hides the deer from view till it's too late, till they're practically on top of you and already running full speed before you see them.

The guys barbecue all week now that Anne has left Ralph. She used to put a roast in the oven some mornings, make a stew others, spend hours peeling potatoes.

The guys never complained about the food, and still don't — just about the smoke, saying it screws with their musk and scares away the deer. Soap's easier for them to avoid than spare ribs.

I've been the youngest in the group since my brother Richard quit hunting two days after he started. Everyone else is Ralph's friend, on a week's holiday from the wife — a few miles away at most, but still away. I use a week's vacation from the plant for this every year but I don't stay the nights, don't even stay for dinner; I go home and get caught up on Susan's day at the bakery, and Nancy's good-but-not-that-good grades, and Mike, too, though after dinner he tends to just do his schoolwork and ignore us. I'm not allowed into the bed or to even sleep on an old blanket on the couch without showering, and when I show up in the mornings at Ralph's it doesn't matter that I haven't shaved or that I've worn the same clothes every day: I still take flak for being the prettiest. That was set to change when Mike came along, though. He was starting to grow but nowhere near needing to shave, not even the few dark hairs above his lip.

The most we could get out of Susan for Mike was Monday, Wednesday and Friday off school, and even that took all we had. She knows better than to complain about the full freezer every winter, but she's never liked that I hunt — never liked that since I was fifteen I've been soaking up all the bullshit the guys sling all week in Ralph's basement, or that for quite a while I soaked up all the rum or whisky or whatever was in the room at the time, too. The guys claim they used to party hard every hunting week, but I realize now that by the time I was old enough to drink they had pretty well settled down—that by the time I quit drinking for good, I was the only one partying every night, the only one bleary-eyed the next morning who might join late and not fully know where in the bush everyone and his muzzleloader were, or just miss the whole day struggling between bed and the toilet.

I stopped spending nights at Ralph's the first November after I quit drinking, and I'd go straight home at the end of the day to help feed and change Mike, help put him to bed. When the night would go quiet and Susan would turn in early I would sit up and read: mysteries, outdated *Macleans*, even Susan's Danielle Steel collection—whatever I could get my hands on. It was a lot like how I used to drink. I missed the guys at Ralph's, but I didn't trust myself. I didn't believe they were really what I missed.

MIKE HAD ALWAYS been in the background with the hunting party, all of them asking all the time, "How long till he gets out here with us?" It was Ralph who asked most, complaining that he barely saw his grandson given all the time he spent on the job in Alberta. The other guys sometimes said the gang could use some new blood, some young legs among the walkers, the guys who fanned out through the trees to sweep the deer toward the blockers waiting at the far edge of the woods to pick off the fleeing beauties.

Mike was in the background with Susan every year, too, who insisted that she didn't want her son involved with guns or stinking up the house Anne had kept so nice or absorbing the so-called wisdom of Ralph's best buddies — so naturally, Ralph just showed up at our door one spring day after Mike turned fifteen, one hand holding the Ministry of Natural Resources license application Mike would need to fill out and the other taking an envelope of cash from his lumberjacket for the safety course fee. I could see Susan's jaw clench when Ralph pushed the money into Mike's hand and said, "Happy birthday." She shot me a look that boiled with hate. Ralph promised Mike a barely used gun was waiting in the cabinet for him in the fall.

Susan and I didn't argue about it after. We didn't need to. Once Ralph got involved in something it happened regardless of whether she or I approved. Mike took the course on Saturdays in August, not seeming to feel her chill in the house those hottest days of the year, and if Susan said anything to him on the weekends she had to drive him, neither of them mentioned it to me. To her credit, I only saw her disapproval in front of Mike once: a rigid "Ask your dad" when he asked her to write him a note for the three days of school he'd miss.

Later, Susan reminded me that I hadn't thought this through, hadn't pictured this fifteen-year-old kid with just a signed piece of paper in his knapsack being sent on his own to explain to a vice-principal why tromping through the bush with a bunch of old farts set on killing deer was a better idea than showing up to math, science or for Chrissakes even English class. I admitted I hadn't considered it. As I had quit school by his age, hunting season hadn't caused a problem for me. I told her I'd call in if Mike got any static from the VP, but good man, he didn't.

WHY NOVEMBER? It's because the deer overpopulate in the summer and breed like rabbits—breed like deer. They gorge on farm crops until the harvest, but then in winter there's not enough food for all of them. We say if they're going to wind up dead and frozen anyway it may as well be in our freezers.

Logic doesn't help the weather, though. It's always cold, wet with rain or snow or mud, and as daylight savings ends the week before, we leave home in the dark in the morning to rally at Ralph's before we drive over the river out of Currie Township and into the neighbouring county, where the deer are penned between the water and the 401.

Ralph hosts something of a meeting the Sunday night before we start, where on the chalkboard on the basement wall he draws a crude map of the next day's terrain. The long arrows from one side represent the walkers, and Xs on the opposite end are blockers. Mike and I missed this, of course—Susan put her foot down about Mike keeping up with school work and sleeping enough to make up for the extra-early mornings in the coming week—but it didn't really matter. I've walked this gully a dozen times, and Monday morning, Ralph made Mike a blocker one station over from himself and said he'd give Mike any help he needed. Then he laughed and said, "Unless we're staring down a big buck. If we've both got a shot, let your old gramps have first crack, would ya?" The poor kid said, "Okay," and I realized no one had really yanked his chain before—at least not the way these guys do it, all of them erupting in laughter when Mike took the bait. Big Al Johnson said after they quieted down, "Don't listen to this blind old bastard. Shoot the fucking thing and put its rack on your wall."

We loaded up three trucks, Mike riding bitch between me and Ralph while four more guys huddled under the topper in the back. We all wore the orange hats and coats the law requires and camo otherwise, Mike's outfit made up of faded and stained pieces other guys got too fat for over the years. We parked at the end of a long dirt lane in a field of corn stubble beside an all-but forgotten cemetery, tiny when seen from the road. There was no snow but the ground was hard, a little white with frost. There'd be mud later.

Ralph went over the plan while we leaned on tailgates and the graveyard's rusty fence. No one needed to hear it except Mike, the first new guy since Richard — or given how that went, the first new guy since me. We split up and I watched Mike ride off with Ralph to set up at the far end of the block. I uncased my gun, its brass patchbox and kickplate still dull on the wooden stock. It only gets used in November weather; I can't be bothered to take apart every piece and polish it like some guys do when the season ends.

The black powder deer hunt is an old-fashioned thing, which for all we piss and moan is what I think we like about it. We'd fill a lot more freezers if we brought our thirty-thirties, but as the province wants population control — not extinction — we set out with our muskets and our bulging canvas bags slung over our shoulders, most of which are just as beat up as the one I've carried since I was Mike's age, when it was new and had yet to take on the vinegary smell of the powder in the rectangular can with the red-tipped spout that gets tilted into a small brass cylinder measure and filled to seventy grains. You stand the gun stock on your foot and send the charge down then take the ramrod from under the barrel and tamp inside till you get a light bounce: packed tight. Next is an oily fabric patch, laid flat atop the bore, then the lead ball on top, then the wooden knob of the ball-starter, which you hit a couple of times before you shove the load to the bottom with the ramrod again.

"Ready?" Gord Roberts asked through his big grey beard. He'd be my partner today, as he had been the last few years. I set the cock to half and made sure there was no percussion cap — no spark — waiting to be struck on the nipple. Caps were in a zipper bag in my satchel to keep them dry. I looked up and said, "Yeah, ready."

We were usually quiet on our way to the bush but today Gord talked some.

"Good to see your boy out."

"Yeah," I said.

"Three generations of Carrions — that's somethin'."

"Huh. Suppose it is."

"Is he ready?"

I had to think about it. Loading the gun in the right order was complicated enough, never mind shooting safely and all Ralph's diagrams and separating the bullshit from the buckwheat with these old coots.

"Hope so," I said. But there was a lot to remember.

I DIDN'T SEE Mike till lunch and even then I didn't talk to him, I only saw him sitting listening to our oldest guy,

Wally Leitch. Ralph was nodding, arms folded, raising a sandwich to his mouth occasionally while Wally rambled. All I could think was, *I hope Mike didn't screw up*. The guys don't go in for surprises. That's what happened with Richard: he took a shot he shouldn't have. Ralph says he heard the ball whizz. It was a short walk that morning, a half-day stalk, and in miserable fog Rich took aim at the first deer he saw — one Ralph had flushed out by himself but hadn't shot at, having the sense to wait till it cleared the brush so as not to hit a blocker. The clean-killed doe didn't matter. At lunch Ralph charged at Rich and with one punch knocked him to the ground.

I hadn't asked Ralph, hadn't thought about it, but it was Rich's gun he lent to Mike. Ralph had bought two on my fifteenth birthday — one for me and one to give to Rich when he was old enough. The twin muskets were a big gesture, part of some *Mice and Men* dream Ralph had briefly had about living off the land or something. He took some time off from the pipeline job and said he was going to spend more time with me and Rich, but he was back out west just two years later. It doesn't make me as angry as it used to — since I quit drinking I've never gotten as angry as I used to — but I think Rich held onto it. He finally moved away two years ago. Nobody seems to have his new number.

WE SAW NO deer before lunch but in the afternoon we heard some rustles, spotted a white tail springing up, bouncing away, a doe with no rack but as Gord's always said, "They're all venison to me." It ran the right way, straight ahead, and a few minutes later it ought to have cleared the woods — God, I *hoped* it cleared the woods — because I heard a shot a good distance ahead. We hustled after it, like we always do when we hear fire. Every man's license lets him tag one deer on the week. We always want to know who's using his.

We emerged from the trees between Mike and Ralph and I called, "Who got that?"

"Not sure," Mike said. He waved his left hand. "That side of Ralph, though."

It was after four and already the sun was setting. One of the guys gathered around had already said he could use a beer and others chimed in that they were up for a whisky, a smoke, dinner, a piss — it all comes out when it's nearly too dark to keep going, sore legs and wet socks and grumbled somethings with *too fuckin' old* in them somewhere.

Wally arrived dragging the carcass and in the fading light stuck his knife into the doe's gut to field dress it. Mike turned his face away. In the truck on the way home he said, "That part was disgusting."

"Didn't they teach you in your course?"

"Yeah," he said. "But I guess didn't think about it — the knife or the blood or what entrails actually are." He looked a little pale.

"When it's your own deer you won't mind."

"I don't know," he said, looking out the window.

WEDNESDAY, MIKE DIDN'T want to get out of bed. After school the day before, he had worked his shift at the

ValuGas then come home and showered and done homework till I don't know when. He was always at the computer in the dining room at night, its one-colour screen lighting his face green and his fingers clicking away at something. Susan said he had some book report due in a week. When I said, "It's still a week away. What's he worried about?" she scowled.

"You and Ralph are asking a lot of him," she said as she pulled the sheets back on the bed.

"We're not asking anything," I said. "What do you mean?"

"I mean he's just doing this to make you happy."

"That's ridiculous. He wants to do this."

She laughed.

"He's near the top of his class in school. He needs to make grades, not to mention money for university. This stupid hunting is a distraction."

"He works so hard. Don't you think he could use a distraction?"

"Lower your voice," she said. "He quit ball. You know how much he loved playing."

"So, now—"

"So now you and Ralph are putting all this pressure on him."

"What—*pressure*?"

"It's pressure. Everything else he's doing is leading him away from here, don't you see?"

"Well, sure, one day, but—"

"Stay out of his way," she said, then almost in a whisper, "He's not like you."

Spitting back the first words that came to mind

would have started something to keep us up all night, so I didn't do it. I rolled one way, Susan rolled the other, and when my alarm went off I crawled out of bed rested and ready for another day, three generations and all that. Mike said thanks for the coffee I handed him in the kitchen when he finally joined me, but that was it — nothing in the car, nothing before he grouped up with Ralph and Wally, who he'd be walking with this morning. I got into Gord's truck and we headed around the block. We'd been walkers the last two days, so we were getting a turn to sit. It's harder to walk every year, and in the last couple some of Ralph's friends have thrown in the towel. Gord was sucking wind pretty hard the day before even if he wouldn't admit it. He still says he prefers to walk, and maybe he does. It's just his body doesn't.

We shot four on the day, all from the blocker end. Mike must have been noisy crashing through the trees, because man did those beauties scatter. Gord got one, and two I took myself, so when the walkers showed up at the end of the afternoon we needed someone's tag. Everyone kind of looked at each other but no one volunteered; if you don't bag a deer in black powder week, your license stays valid to bow-hunt the rest of the winter.

"Mike?" Ralph said.

Without hesitating, Mike said, "Yeah, no problem."

Ralph asked him and me to ride up front with him on the way back.

"Mike, you should have offered your tag," Ralph said.
"I did."
"He means before anyone asked you," I added quietly.
"Uh … Okay."

He's a sharp kid, I think he got it. I could have left it there.

Ralph couldn't.

"You know, you're the new guy," he said. "You have to show everyone you want to be part of the team. They may not know what to think of you yet. You've got to integrate. Okay?"

"Okay," Mike said again.

Ralph looked away from the road, at me. "I mean, you guys don't even come for dinner. And Mike, these guys don't know you at all."

Mike snapped, "Nope, they don't." He didn't even look sideways, just straight out the windshield.

"You made your point, Dad," I said.

I couldn't remember the last time I'd called Ralph "Dad".

Ralph let out a heavy breath and said, "All right. But come for dinner tonight, for Chrissakes. We got steaks."

I thought Susan might kill us, but I agreed.

Mike didn't say anything the rest of the way.

"So it ... is ... *pouring*," Wally said from the old brown couch in the basement. He was telling the story of the buck on the rainy day again. That beauty had kept getting bigger over the years, and the rain had kept falling harder. The legend had been growing since before I started hunting.

"You remember the big gully from Monday?" Wally asked.

Mike nodded. Someone had given him a beer that sat

on the cement floor beside his armchair, almost out of sight. I pretended it was.

"Well, that's where we were. The trees were a lot younger then, and the mud ran down the hill that much more, but them walkers, they were at least a little protected. Me, I was just sittin' and gettin' *soaked*, waitin' around in weather *people* are usually too smart to go out in, never mind a fuckin' deer." He looked up at me after his F-word; I gave a small head-shake and smiled. "So anyway, I'm just mindin' my own business. It's still early in the mornin', still practically dark, and this deer comes up out of nowhere—"

"Like a ghost, right?" Big Al called over.

Gord said, taunting, "A will-o-the-wisp, maybe?"

Wally raised a finger and said, "You weren't there."

"Neither was that big buck!" Al shouted. Everyone laughed.

"Don't listen to them, young fella." Wally sipped his whiskey and fixed on Mike. "So like I said, this buck shows up, easily a twelve-point, rack wider than"—he spread his arms like a toddler who loves you *this* much —"and he just walks up and just stands there. I didn't need to shoot, even, coulda just knocked him in the head with the gun stock. But he's *so* close, I can't even move—I'd scare him away, right?"

"What did you do?" Mike asked.

"Uh-oh," Gord said just to me, smiling through his whiskers. "Kid's hooked." I took a drink from my glass of water. Wouldn't matter what was in my hand, I'd drink it here.

"I just waited," Wally said. "The rain's comin' down

in fuckin' sheets, big fat strips of it, mud every fuckin' place, and all I can do is look at the thing. And he's lookin' back. We sit there, I don't know, must be ten minutes, then he walks ahead of me, nice and slow. Just goes about his day like anybody else."

"Here we go," Ralph said, having just entered with a fresh bowl of chips.

"So finally I get out a cap as slow as I can and put it on the nipple. I cock the gun and I lift it up. He's dead at twenty yards, nothin' to it. I squeeze the trigger ... and just, *click*. Hammer hits the cap, but the damned thing doesn't go off."

"Seriously," Mike said.

"Seriously. So I don't know, I think it's a bad cap, maybe wet from the rain. I take out another one, put it on, aim and shoot again. Nothin'. So now what — I've got to disassemble the gun and pull the ball." Wally laughed a little. "Can't do it there, though."

"Shit," Mike said softly. I heard him, but I wouldn't say anything anymore.

"That's not even the best part," Wally said.

Gord laughed. "It's the best part that actually happened."

"It's all true, Michael," Wally said.

Gord again: "Nah it ain't!"

"I'm telling you, Michael: my buck looked back at me and he winked before he walked away. Didn't even run — just sauntered off like he had all day." Wally started to laugh, then. "He takes two or three steps out and I just hear, *BLAM!*"

Ralph started laughing, too, eyeing Mike a second

then pointing up at the wall over the chalkboard. There's been a deer skull mounted there as long as I can remember, with a tiny set of antlers, four points, maybe — a young male, but still a male. Mike stood up and squinted at the gold-coloured plate on the wood backing.

It reads: "Wally's Buck."

"It was a different deer," Wally said.

"Yeah, the hell it was!" everybody chorused with Ralph.

I knew this was coming, of course. They had choreographed the routine for me when I was Mike's age but I had taken it differently: I was embarrassed and angry at how they had strung me along. But in all the years since, I hadn't gotten to use it on Rich or anybody until Mike. From the chair I was in tonight, it was a hell of a lot of fun.

Mike took it in stride, I think. "It's like fishing stories," he said with a shrug on the ride home. "They're always bullshit."

I felt myself smiling. I thought maybe he was even enjoying this.

FRIDAY, AS THE day wound down. Mike hadn't been gung-ho in the morning, but had soldiered on after all last night's schoolwork. Ralph had assigned him to block, separating me and Mike again, but before we split up at the edge of the woods I said, "Dammit, Ralph, I brought my son hunting and I haven't spent a minute with him yet." Ralph said, kind of huffy-like, "All right, block with Mike." He lifted one leg and bent his knee a couple of times. "Yeah, I can walk today," he added. He had to get his dig in somewhere.

From where we set up we could see a farm in the distance and beyond that the 401—far enough away that we probably couldn't put a ball through anyone's window or worse, but I reminded Mike nonetheless: "We take sure shots here." We took up separate positions maybe fifty yards apart in the long grass, facing the point where the bush met the field. Half the corn crop still stood, too underdeveloped after a cool summer to finish harvesting. Deer love it, but none came that morning—or maybe they did, we just couldn't see them. They don't know they're hiding when they go to feed. Noon had passed and I had eaten my sandwich before two streaked out from the stalks, broadside to us and well under seventy yards away. They slowed a little and down the line of blockers from the left, three shots banged. I was fourth. The startled deer high-tailed it farther to the right and into the woods. I listened for Mike, next in line.

No shot.

From my left the guys stepped out of the brush into the field. You have to talk about the action anytime you get any, and while you do the rest of the deer in the woods laugh at you then run the other way. Killing the deer might be the least important part, though.

I looked right. Mike still hadn't emerged. I called his name and finally heard a slight rustle. He pushed his way out of the weeds, not even bothering to bring his gun. He scratched his neck with one hand. He looked into the distance a minute, at the farm we all hoped was far enough away.

"You get a shot?" I asked, but I knew the answer.

"Didn't like the look of the house behind," he mumbled.

Wally joined us from the station left of me.

"You'll get 'em next year." He laughed. "Mine's still out there, too, y'know."

"Yeah," Mike said.

I nodded and said, "Right choice," but I had seen Mike like this so many mornings just after he had woken up: the droopy face, the dopey voice, I recognized it all. He had to have known I knew, too, but I never did mention it. He'd never get Wally's buck—none of us would—and he'd decide against hunting the next year, too, saying he couldn't miss school. In the end he'd never come with us again. For now, though, till the sun went down, there was still a little time: a couple more hours with the bullshit, and Mike was starting to get the hang of it.

Swept Up

I.

I SIGNED UP FOR drama because it's the one class where they don't teach anything. I knew I'd have to do the play in late spring, but I didn't care because no one I knew would come see it. We were doing *Our Town* and when I asked Mr. Lenders why he cast me as the Stage Manager character who narrates most of the show, he said he thought I could do it, but much more importantly, that I *would* do it. A couple of guys hated me for it because they were already playing the achievement game, investing heavily in local renown and expecting it to pay out. The part could have helped them meet a girl and get married, have kids and get divorced one day or not but be miserable regardless.

DAD HADN'T SAID much the last few months, and all Mom was saying lately was that driving into Currie four nights a week to pick me up from rehearsal was a pain. I was staying late even on the days when my scenes weren't scheduled, but I had to know what tone was being set before I walked on. If that sounds like I committed, you're right. I did. When I first announced the part to Dad, his glare made up my mind.

Mom's reaction was to giggle condescendingly and remind me how, just a few years before, I hadn't even wanted to walk across the stage at Grade Eight graduation. She got that wrong: I hadn't wanted to go at all. It wasn't an achievement, and neither was *Our Town*; to get the course credit, everyone had to do the show, just like it had been when Mom was in school. Her class had done *The Crucible*, and she had wanted to play Elizabeth Proctor. On one of our rides home, she told me it was just as well that she hadn't gotten the role, as her Proctor was a jock who had a girlfriend already and on top of that, by the time she went on stage her pregnancy weight was helping fill out her baggy costume as Tituba, the servant she was cast to play in blackface in the opening scene. Mr. Johanssen — my principal, her history teacher — burst into the classroom where the girls were changing minutes before the first show and forbid Mom to wear the dark makeup, though the way she saw it, Johanssen was just trying to see the girls in their underwear. She said she flubbed her opening line because of all the commotion, as though Johanssen was the one who had cost her the chance to get out of Currie Township and as far away as her talent would take her, which in my estimation then was about fourteen kilometres down 402, not even to London, pulled over on the shoulder with a flat. But these are the grudges we hold.

Mom was happy I was doing the show. Anytime we

talked about it front of Dad, though, he flopped his wrist in front of his chest and lisped *dramma* like it rhymed with *grandma*. I didn't bother correcting him, there was no point anymore. His gibes at me were the most he said to anyone.

II.

I HAD THE biggest part so I was last in the curtain call, and the crowd — eighty people opening night, it felt like the whole town — stood and clapped its loudest for me before giving us all an ovation. I doubt we deserved it, but in the front row were the students' council try-hards who had witnessed this behaviour a week before when they scammed their way onto our class trip to *Death of a Salesman* at the Grand Theatre in London. Mr. Lenders told us he thought *Death* had more to say and that he'd have mounted it were the cast not so small; he didn't want us drama students building sets and rigging lights in place of shop class co-ops, though they just dicked around and called us *fucking queers* most of the time, anyway.

MR. LENDERS HAD changed the script so that our town wasn't in New Hampshire anymore, but right here in Currie, and these weren't the only notes on my script; every rehearsal, I had marked up not just lines but actions along with them: *Take two steps. Raise arm. Pause for laugh.* Sometimes my private stage directions even covered intonations. *Wistful. Sigh. Deadpan.* The only way I knew to conjure he who wasn't me was to use consistent, planned actions, like checking off a list, an approach rendered useless in the third act when Stella Callaghan, in the role of Emily Webb, started actually crying. For three months of rehearsal she'd tried to squeeze out just a tear or two when her character had to finally leave ~~Grover's Corners~~ Currie behind, only to be surprised that first night when a flood of them finally came. My volume fell along with her faltering voice, as did the rest of the cast's, while black-clad Lenders nearly tugged his earlobe off at the back of the gym repeating the universal sign for *Can't hear you.* I don't think the back rows knew how the play ended but in front they ate it up, hence the ovation. The lights came on and Mom and Dad rose from somewhere in the middle, applauding and cheering, and in the car on the way home they told me I'd been fantastic and that they hadn't realized, even Mom, just how many lines I had and how I must have programmed every step, every pause, every everything. I shrugged them off and said Mr. Lenders was a good teacher, when really I had learned from the masters: here they were praising me together at the right moment, choosing their words and facial expressions and tones of voice to show a united front.

Or maybe they just got swept up in it.

III.

DAD LEFT ONE week after the play closed, on a Saturday afternoon while I was working my new job at the Price-Mart. Our family of four stayed up late the night before in the lawn chairs around the backyard fire pit where nothing burned tonight. Dad broke the news, and when Nancy started crying Mom led her to the house. It was just me and Dad then, and I had gotten too old: he would have to explain. He lit up a cigarette and offered the pack.

"No thanks," I said, though I could have used one.

He laughed.

"Already smarter than me," he said. "You'll be fine."

"Why should I have to be?"

He avoided my eyes.

"You know, your mother and I," he began. "We didn't really choose this."

"No," I said. "*You're* leaving *her*."

He put his hands together then spread them apart, finishing with his arms wide.

"I mean *this*," he said. I looked at him but he still wouldn't look back. "Mortgage, family, booster shots, grass to cut—it all just sort of happened."

My eyes stretched. Blood rushed to my face.

"You're saying you never *wanted* us?"

He didn't answer.

"Goddammit! Why won't you look at me?"

He faced me and his stare was empty.

"You can at least be a man about it," I said. "Look me in the eye and say you don't want me."

He cleared his throat.

"Your mother ..."

"Me!"

"You, and your sister, and your mother," he said, "are the best thing that ever happened to me. I didn't choose it, but that doesn't mean I didn't want it."

"You just don't anymore."

"I just want to choose," he said, finally making eye contact. "I choose you, I choose your sister. I want to stay in your lives and everything—"

He looked at the ground.

"But?"

"But your mother ..."

I turned away and let slip a loud disgusted breath.

"I never said no to her once in my life," he said. "Since we rode the school bus together, since she tried her damnedest to tutor me. She pulled me along the whole way. So when things fell apart with your father ..."

"*You're* my father."

He smiled.

"No," he said. "I'm not."

"You taught me how to field a ground ball, and how to chop wood with an axe, and ..."

"You'll never need those things," he said. He shook his head.

"What are you talking about?" I asked.

"You already know there aren't many options here."

"So ..."

"So you're already choosing," he said. "It's not too late for you."

His mouth was slightly open in a pained expression, and the outer corners of his eyes looked heavy. I'd wake up in the morning and Mom would drive me into Currie for work again. By the time I got home, he'd be gone. He butted out his cigarette and offered his hand. That was it, a handshake. I gripped it—firmly without squeezing, like he'd taught me.

"You neither," I said. He got up and went into the house, and once all the lights were out, so did I.

IV.

ONE OF THOSE afternoons when I was riding home with Mom, a tornado crossed Seventeen between Currie and Waubnakee. At the end of a long laneway it tore the roof off a giant pig barn and left pink insulation clouds in the trees behind and scrap metal in the corn stubble all the way to the road. Mom stopped the car on the shoulder and we gawked at the pickup trucks convening near the gate. Overweight, suspender-wearing farmers formed a circle and whistled and swore, arriving one after another until eventually Mom put the car back into gear and we drove on saying nothing as the sky thundered and rain pummelled the windshield. We stopped where Seventeen met Highway 2 and the red sign was four feet in diameter. It had been replaced with a bigger one every time someone had been T-boned there, and now a red light blinked atop it day and night as did others in a box on wires above the intersection, red for Seventeen, amber for Two. We looked left and right and then we drove through, officially into Waubnakee.

On the front lawns along Main Street, whole soaked families lined the cracked sidewalks, surveying the clouds. Mom slowed as someone approached the car—Ernestine, my eighty-year-old great-great-aunt. We stopped and I rolled down my window as she hobbled up, losing her perm in the weather.

"Didn't you hear?" she asked, creaky voice straining over rain and wind.

"No," Mom said.

"Tornado warning: Waubnakee and Western Currie Township."

I laughed and said, "Gee, thanks," then cranked my window closed. Mom flashed me a dirty look as she stepped off the brake. The car resumed its slow roll home, and I knew: no matter how big the sign, these people would never stop.

The Expiry Dates

20 AL 97

MY EYES FLIT from Ron to the corkboard on his wall, just long enough to think: *What has to go wrong in a man's life? When does he decide that moving to Currie Township and opening a Giant Tiger store is a good idea?*

And he says: "I should hire you."

My eyes flit back.

"Uh, pardon?"

"Why should I hire you?" he repeats. Tiny beads of sweat form under my shirt. *Did I just hear what I wanted to hear? Is that what I wanted to hear?*

"My experience," I say.

Oh, good one. You're a seventeen-year-old kid.

In person, Ron must see how young I am. That I couldn't have been sixteen when I started at Bevan Eggs. That there's no way my résumé should also list a gas station or the Price-Mart, soon to be Currie's lesser grocery store, where all I had to know was how to rotate by expiry date.

1. Take the old eggs off the shelf.
2. Put the new eggs on.
3. Bury the new with the old.

I started at Price-Mart in September, so now I've learned to rotate yogurt. And cheese. And milk. But I've also learned the really important stuff about working. Show up on time, don't call in sick if you're not dead and most importantly, don't talk about people behind their backs. They always find out. Or at least the Tremblay twins on cash did, that time the butcher counter guys asked me who I thought was hotter, leaving aside that they're my third cousins, of course — everyone in Currie Township probably is. I said Aurore, someone told Angèle, and now here I am applying at Giant Tiger, impressing Ron somehow by shutting up at "experience".

The silence hangs a moment, until he says "Well, all right," and moves on to the next question.

"Why is it important to pull the older stock forward on the shelf?"

This is too easy.

22 AL 97

THE PHONE RINGS in the afternoon, and when I pick up, Ron hires me. Mom drives me to the first meeting, where Ron welcomes me and the other fifty-three employees to Giant Tiger Two-Forty-Two, Currie, Ontario.

Ron talks through his moustache about goal-setting then points out the section bosses. The last is a shaggy young redhead named Ivan, who will supervise me in the Grocery Department. They needed introduction, but almost everyone else is from Currie High School. I even recognize someone like Sharon Foster, who's a year older than me and repeating Grade Twelve math, because even the most unremarkable girl in school can't be invisible here. Everyone from Currie goes to CHS, and so do all the farm kids from Currie Township. The only ones who don't are the Catholic kids, who lived beside us in grade school then went missing around puberty.

I can see them again tonight, though. I can prove they're real.

Currie has Catholic School Girls.

I met Katrina first, the dark-haired, dark-eyed Polish-born figure skater; then, Catrina, the dark-haired, dark-eyed Portuguese-born figure skater; and after her, Megan Cavanagh, who spent half of Grade Nine at CHS before changing to the Catholic system and the infamous six a.m. bus to London. Who has tiny blonde curls that fall over the arms of her glasses. Who has miniscule, not-quite-separated fingers from being born premature. (And who clearly figure skates, though she doesn't mention it.) All three work in Ladies' Wear with den mother Tonja, the curvy immigrant who taught me the first night (while pointing to another new hire) that, "In Hungary, you never see woman in just T-shirt and sweat pant."

Sadly for Tonja, in Currie you do.

20 MA 97

THE FIRST FEW weeks have been easy work:

1. *Wait for a shelf to be built.*
2. *Find out which unsellable GT Brand product it holds.*
3. *Stock it.*

4. Resume waiting. Or flirting. Or whatever it is you're doing to pass the time.

At ten this morning, a Saturday, Currie's first security guard stands aside. Its first automatic doors slide open and let half the town in, led by a blur of curly grey hair. The woman's features come into focus when she stops at the till, making history by grabbing at a cellophane bag of powdery strawberry candies.

"It's Marlene Simmons," she snarls, hoisting her trophy for the *Seed-Tribune* photographer. "I bought the first thing from this store." She tosses the sweets on the counter and adds: "Gimme a pack of Craven A's, too."

Marlene leaves with the first signature yellow shopping bag and smokes her cigarette outside the sliding doors. Moments later she re-enters pushing a cart, nerves calmed, her shopping bag nestled where a baby could have sat.

30 NO 97

Vaughan's Bakery closed last year, but not before Nancy and I had spent countless Saturdays there, reading on the hard wooden chairs while Dad worked overtime at the plant. When Mom had to leave the counter for the backroom, I'd play shopkeeper and greet her best customers, all grandmothers, until she returned to rescue them.

I must have absorbed something. At the first-ever Giant Tiger Christmas Party, Ron presents three Customer Service Awards. Greg Watkins called an ambulance for an old lady who had a heart attack in Housewares. In Menswear, Maria, a squat lifer in the making, is already the Portuguese community's woman on the inside. And when Ron cites two comment cards saying *Mike's so kind*, I win the third one. I don't recall trying to be kind but I take it.

05 JA 98

MY LAST SEMESTER of OAC starts Monday. I've been going out with Brandy Crawford for a year but there's no way I'm taking her to prom. She doesn't have a job, for one, and she keeps failing her driver's test. And since Dad left in his roaring Cutlass and abandoned a shitbox Pontiac 6000 *that was such a good deal*, it's been me who's had to take Brandy to the mall in London all the time to go shopping. She always says she'll pay me back but I've lost track of how much she owes me.

Like Megan, Catrina and Katrina, Brandy's a year behind me in school. She tells me every day that she hates Megan, despite having never met her, and it doesn't help that Brian fooled around with Katrina-with-a-K on New Year's.

Brian works at the store now, too; when Greg went off to college, I put the good word in. Other than spending more time chatting up Catrina-with-a-C than Ron would like, Brian does all right, and Tonja, who's married, has even extended him the same, increasingly serious "Be my boy toy" offers she's always given me.

Sometimes Brian and I have coffee and smokes at Don's after work and then follow each other around the county roads in the dark. When he has his mom's Mercury, he drops his window to remind me about its four-point-six litre V8 before he peels out and vanishes in the night. I caught him once, but I jumped the CN tracks going one-eighty to do it.

23 MA 98

ALL MONTH OUR grade's been raving about how drunk we're getting Two-Four Weekend. Most of us are still underage, but we've all spent five years in the same classes. Kyle Hall's next bush bash is all that's left to talk about.

Kyle's a bassist in two bands. One begs to perform at every school assembly, and the other incants *clarinet scholarship* and makes lonely, kind-of-pretty girls disappear from Currie Township forever. Megan's his date, but when Brandy and I rumble up with Brian — in the decrepit van, this time — she's already by herself, leaning on an oak and drinking a cooler. From the backseat, before Brian even turns off the key, Brandy starts going on about what a skank Megan is and says to me, "You've become a flirt," when she gets a glimpse of *what goes on at work*, as she calls it. She spends our half-hour at the party glaring over my shoulder, making faces and repeatedly flipping Megan off, and when Megan laughs too hard at something I say, Brandy punches her in the face and snaps the bridge of her glasses. She runs straight to the van after, giving Brian and me no choice but to follow; he sprays gravel and we leave Megan's girlfriends in the laneway shrieking at our tail lights. I nearly fall out as I heave the sliding door. When it closes with a thud I know Giant Tiger will never be the same.

07 JL 98

BRANDY AND I broke up a month ago, but it had nothing to do with Megan. I just outgrew the relationship. Besides, Megan's with Stephen now, this blond wiener who transferred to the Currie store when his parents moved here from London. He's younger and he's looking to replace me. Seriously. He runs around the store stocking shelves — *sometimes actually running* — and his mop and bucket find accidents faster than an ambulance. I caught him making siren sounds once, but otherwise, he's good: he never gets busted with Megan. Not that I mind. He can have her, and for all I care he can have Giant Tiger, too. I got into university and I start in the fall.

Inventory in June pushed back our one-year reviews, so today is my first crack at a good, but not *too* good, self-evaluation. I complete my form in the break room and make my way downstairs.

Instead of the usual power-figure-behind-a-desk look, the manager's office is laid out with a bank of three computers at the back. Ron shuts the door. He pushes a chair into the centre of the room — an island for me — and then he sits at his work station. He scans the page and chortles.

"First things first," he says. "I don't give five out of five."

I set my jaw.

"Read the questions."

"All right." He sighs and sets the paper on the desk. "We'll go through them one by one."

I wheel in beside him and look over his shoulder. He reads the first checkbox.

"Presentation. Clean uniform. Hair, and, if applicable,

facial hair well-groomed." He pauses. "You gave yourself five."

I meet his eye and dare him to look. My hair is cut short and gelled in place. I shave redundantly before every shift. Today my black Giant Tiger golf shirt is fresh from the wash.

Ron takes the bait. He puts pen to paper.

"That's a five," I say.

He glowers through his puny glasses. His forehead wrinkles but his face softens.

"Well, I suppose I can give you *one* five," he says. "Uniform. Always worn, complete with name tag."

"That's a five too, Ron." He doesn't argue. I take four out of five in the rest of the categories—only fair since I've started coming in late every day—and I return to the floor. Just my luck, I meet Stephen in the doorway. Of course he started just in time for evaluations. Of course he's being lumped into this round. Of course Ron will give him the one-year raise early.

21 SE 98

BEYOND TONJA AND Maria, and the figure skaters, and me, two originals remain. Ivan is still running Grocery, and Sharon's made a home of cash six. Since leaving high school, Ivan's smoked so much pot that he *likes* this job, and since last winter, he's been dating Sharon, who's in her second year at Western. She and I crossed paths on campus yesterday, and she invited me to a mixer tonight.

Before pulling into my laneway, she straightened her light brown hair and put concealer over her too many freckles. As she shifts into drive her slender collarbone crests the V-neck of her sweater. She smiles when I ask to switch from Hitz Radio to the campus station. When we finally have to say something else, she tells me she and Ivan had a fight.

At the Drips, London's oldest dive bar, Sharon and I dance, and we drink, and we introduce ourselves as *just friends*. Neither one of us should drive after last call, but I'm in better shape so I offer. When she refuses I collapse on the passenger seat.

There are never any cops on Old 22, but *to be extra safe*, Sharon says, we turn down a dirt road just outside the city. The farm fields grow longer, and darker, and emptier. Each is more desolate than the last. We ride quietly until the only sound, the motor's gentle hum, gives way to crunching gravel.

Sharon stops the car. She looks down at her lap.

"You're right," she says. "You should drive."

We step out in front of the headlights to switch seats. We fall onto the hood together.

25 SE 98

I ASK SHARON out for the coming weekend. She says *Friday was fun, but ...*

28 SE 98

IVAN QUIT GIANT Tiger yesterday. Ron doesn't talk to me anymore. And everyone seems to have forgotten that Stephen and Megan got caught making out behind the box-baler last month: Golden Boy's already the new Grocery Manager, and a shoo-in for one of the Customer Service Awards. The other two will go to employees who catch people shoplifting. The award's name won't reflect the change.

Brian and Katrina are off-again, for good. In August he took a job installing carpets, and he's been talking about *going army* ever since. A buzz-cut tenth-grader named Will took his place, and on his first shift I noticed him already chafing under Stephen's micro-management. Immediately I took Will under my wing and taught him who he could tease, who to stay away from, and of course, a wide range of deniable misdeeds that make Golden Boy crazy. Mostly we just slit open expired cold cut packs and bury them in the tallest, fullest skids of new stock. Will works Mondays before school and gets the payoff, watching Stephen smell the rot and check side-to-side for Ron before he mutters, "Fucking weekend guys," and sets to work off-loading the pallet. Every Friday night, when I come in, I head straight for the expired stock again with my box cutter.

01 NO 98

I DRIVE TO London for class every day, and I'm down to four hours a week, so today I hand Ron the letter. He coaxes lame applause from my last pre-shift meeting and makes a show of thanking me, *for two years' service*. It's barely eighteen months but I don't correct him. He goes on to air-quote the *bigger and better things* I'm *moving onto* but doesn't name them, which implies I actually said this. I didn't. Only Will asks what the *things* are. He has two years left at CHS, but last week, when Stephen transferred back to London—he and Megan are engaged now—Ron promoted Will to Grocery Manager. On a life total of six weeks' experience.

I spend my final night expressly not working, and for my big exit I turn a cartwheel past Ron and run out the sliding doors. The air is cold, the season's changing. I don't look back at the strip mall. As I walk to the 6000 I hear Will's voice.

"Hey, Mike!"

He's the last person I'll speak to at Giant Tiger. So be it.

"I got a date with Catrina Friday," he says as he approaches the car. "In case I don't see you beforehand," Will continues, as though I'm coming back tomorrow. "You've known her a while …"

I get in and shut the door hard. Turn the key. Click the shifter into drive. Behind me, the sign's stupid grin goes dark, and in the rear-view Will's invisible now. I toe the brake and wash him in red light. He approaches and I can't decide whether I'm proud or embarrassed for him. I lower the glass and he offers his hand. My eyes stay glued to the console. Campus radio crackles in faintly. I twist the volume to *MAX* so he leans in and shouts.

"Can't you give me *any* advice?"

I close my eyes and wish for power windows. Then I punch the gas.

Precision

*E*VERYTHING CAME DOWN to the jacket: blue nylon, white stitching, CFSC across the back for Currie Figure Skating Club and my name, Jessie, in script on the arm. In high school it separated me from the pack, and around town, it sometimes got me mistaken for a popular girl, one who skated solo and who the club sent to London for development camp every August—the one who spent the rest of the season quoting *Kurt* and *Liz* and *Elvis* like her one-day guest teachers had been close friends.

That girl was Megan Cavanagh, and in our last season she still hadn't grown past five feet. She had precious blonde curls and when she skated, she traded eyeglasses for contacts. Every program she turned three perfect double axels. She fell every time she practiced the triple, but regardless she ditched us for the Forest City Diamonds that October. We knew they'd never let her skate singles in London, but as part of their Precision team she'd skate circles around us.

It's not quite a sport, and not quite a pageant, and Precision is a stupid name because there's always that imprecise person tucked out of sight in the back, like the guys who can't dance—all the guys—in the Currie

Community Theatre musicals. That girl was me, making up the points my skills lost with my petroleum-jellied smile and hairsprayed-down skirt. I hung on till the max age, twenty-one, Senior Double A—I was driving back from Fanshawe College for practices—and even that year, I walked the moist-aired arena hallway smelling the French fries and feeling the familiar half-hope, half-dread butterflies, unsure which half went with *made the team* or *cut*. In no particular order (my mom, the coach, always said), Megan was atop the list again and I was twentieth. No one begrudged Megan—it wasn't her spot they were after—but the girls who didn't see their names hated me for barely scraping through and went home in tears and bitched, *Of course Jessie made the team.* It wasn't my fault, though: every summer another skater left town or got pregnant or grew overnight into the massive farm girl her mother had long been, leaving me holding the last pair of hips once again, turning the four-spoke wheel out from the centre face-off dot.

It's called Precision because there are twenty bodies on the ice, which is more than a hockey game, counting even the referees. If you're not where you're supposed to be a collision's a risk, knee-on-knee or head-to-head and you're not wearing pads. The boys who play hockey know how much those hurt; the boys who figure skate, less so, but by age seven most have traded toe picks and leather for sticks and skates with hard boots, and intermission performances for three sweaty periods. The only boy who didn't was Brian Callaghan, and he was the best skater we had—better than Megan, even. His parents argued with the club executive for a few seasons, demanding to know why a boy couldn't be on the Precision team, but eventually they dropped it, to Brian's relief. He was already the club workhorse, partner to every girl who skated pairs, and in addition to his singles program he cooked up wacky rock-and-roll routines for the end-of-year fundraiser. When he was thirteen, he slicked his blond hair back and his mom altered an old pair of his dad's black jeans. They were too big in the crotch but close everywhere else, and behind giant black sunglasses he vamped his way around the oval to *Pretty Woman*. My age group waited to perform next, and when he skated past us at the corner of the rink he pointed at me, tongue curled for the *Rrrowr*. It hit me in the throat and sent a charge through my body suit—along the seams, around the hips, down to where they met in the middle.

Brian lived for the year-end show because he'd never stood a chance against the Diamonds; while their boys had been protected through Montessori schools and Children's Museum memberships, Brian was general population in Currie. He quit skating in Grade Nine after an ass-whupping at lunch hour, when Chad Mitchell, captain of every other team at our high school, dragged him out of the cafeteria to the smoking pit where he and a few other meatheads bruised Brian's ribs and bloodied his face the way Chad would later bloody mine. Brian didn't answer when they taunted, "You still feel pretty?" and for a long time he didn't say another word about figure skating.

Of course that was the first year that I was asked to skate pairs; I'd had my growth spurt young, but all the other girls had caught up, so now I was back among the shortest and the lightest, bigger than only Megan but without the talent. They had scheduled me into Brian's strong hands and I was ready for him to lift me, but as our first practice had been set for the day after the beating, he didn't speak of me again, either.

IN OUR LAST season, Megan slipped during the Diamonds' closing block as she moved into the twentieth position. She wasn't better than me at that. We didn't win the meet, but we finished ahead of Forest City for the first time, so Mom called the fire department to get the trucks for a parade like the hockey teams had every year no matter where they finished in Tri-County, (usually first), or how they fared in Regionals against a London team, (one upset win ever, thirty years ago, that Hank still talks about).

People say Hockey and Skating support each other because on Friday night, at the last-place Junior C Comets' games, the Precision team emerges from hockey-stinking dressing rooms to perform between periods while everyone's rushing to the upstairs lounge to chug a beer. And on hockey parade days, the Senior Double A girls still line the street wearing club jackets over their bodysuits and full competition makeup: bright exaggerated eye shadow, the reddest possible lips and criminal amounts of blush. As the sirens sound, we smile and blow kisses to the boys no matter whether they're seven-year-old Novices or teenage Juveniles — guys not even good enough for the Comets — because for these boys, this will be as good as it gets. None will leave town for a better team like Megan did. Most won't leave for college. Most won't leave at all.

We finally got the fire trucks on a Tuesday afternoon, not a Saturday morning like the hockey players did, and some of us couldn't even get the time off work. Those who did show up laughed and hugged and cried a little at the fire hall; we'd skated our whole lives, and this was the end of it. We climbed on board and the siren wailed, but when we turned onto Main Street we saw virtually no one, just the *Seed-Tribune* photographer, our parents, and Brian, in his way-too-small-now Club jacket, which was wet from the shoulder down the front. At his feet was the McDonalds cup thrown from the passing car. They probably yelled, *Faggot!* too. He stood his ground, though, applauding anyway, and when he caught my eyes and returned my wave with a giant smile, I felt my cheeks flush. Then I blushed more, embarrassed that I had.

Our picture ran in the paper the next week with the caption *Victory Parade*. The Juveniles hit on us at Brewskie's the weekend after, saying they were sorry they'd missed it and offering us our kisses now, dropping to their knees and head-butting our thighs as we squirmed away. Most of us giggled and swatted playfully, but I left a bright red handprint on Mitchell's cheek.

Brian sat apart from it, neither one of them nor one of us, in the little booth in the front corner with a high seatback that blocks the window, shadows all but hiding him from the rest of the bar. He sat there every Friday night, and Saturdays, too, with his pick of girls from the skating club. It was Brandy Crawford that night, youngest on our team — barely nineteen, though it's not like Brewskie's checks.

Brandy dumped Brian's best friend, Mike, for spending too much time hitting on Megan when they worked at the GT together — that's not how Mike told it, though, after he and I had each moved to London and he began answering my calls after the bars closed and turning up at my place a half-hour later. I used to see him at Brewskie's, too, when everyone came home for Thanksgiving and Christmas, but most times he'd be so smashed with Brian that I'd stop drinking so I could drive them home, shuddering and flooring the gas when I passed the house I grew up in, where Hank still lived, alone.

It was a different story other weekends, when I came back to Currie for no specific occasion and stayed in the apartment my best friend Stella shared with her boyfriend Wade. Brewskie's would fill on Fridays as always, and Brian would wait in the corner booth for the next girl to come to him, taking the extra step now of covering his lap and hers with her skating club jacket, hiding the hands that could have raised me as they instead dove under a waistband and produced drunken coos and heavy breathing.

THE LAST TIME I saw it happen, the girl was Megan; she was back living at her parents' place after her perfect fiancé Stephen changed his mind and enrolled at St. Peter's Seminary. I pointed her out as she climbed off Brian's lap and smoothed her skirt as though no one knew, the idiot.

"Whatever," Stella said. "Fucking slut."

"Mike was so in love with her," I said. "How could they do that?"

Stella laughed.

"Mike missed his chance." She narrowed her eyes. "Besides, what do you care? You've got him right where you want him."

I felt my cheeks redden.

"It's nothing," I said. "Really. I don't want Mike."

"So what ... you just hate Megan?"

I shook my head, laughing a little.

"I don't care about Megan."

Stella's expression froze, eyebrows raised, mouth half-open.

"Brian?" she said. "*My little brother?*"

I exhaled.

"Yeah."

She put a hand on my shoulder.

"Give it up, Jess."

"What?" I felt myself getting angry. "We're grown-ups now ... I mean, it wouldn't *bother* you ... would it?"

She shook her head.

"It's not that," she said. "Go get off in the booth if you want. But he's leaving town next week. He joined the army."

I looked at Brian and pictured him in khaki green everything, T-shirts and baggy pants and the four-season jacket he'd wear even on his own time. He'd get screamed at for six straight weeks of training then ship out to some garrison town, where he'd go to a bar a lot like Brewskie's with a new crop of Megans in corner booths like this one.

"Why'd he do that?" I asked.

"He can't stay here anymore," Stella said.

It rushed in on me.

"But the booth, with the girls ...?"

She laughed.

"So nobody knows?" I asked.

She shook her head.

"Just our family — and my parents will never tell."

"Did they kick him out?"

"Not exactly," Stella said. "They're glad it's the army, though. My dad thinks killing a man could straighten him out."

"That's ridiculous," I said.

"I know." She smiled a little. "Brian's always been best with clear objectives, though. Like in skating. And he's always been so competitive. He'll love keeping score at the range."

In my mind I watched him robotically shoot targets now, bull's-eye every time while I missed mine completely. The last-call bell rang and I walked over and said goodbye to him with a quick hug and a peck on the cheek, so obviously not sexual for him and never would be. I drove back to the city instead of staying the night, and when I got in I called Mike but he didn't answer this time. I crawled into bed and as I turned out the lamp, the last thing I saw was my club jacket. I shut my eyes but it was still there, hanging limply from the hook on the closet door.

Comets

WADE WORKS IN the yard at Gable's Nursery, transplanting shrubs and lugging seed bags to the cars in the lot. He shows up every morning in the same grubby Aerosmith T-shirt, but the weather's so humid that by ten he's draped it over a fencepost. I watch him the same way I did that first summer, muscles flexed taut in his arms and his chest, six-pack and V-lines pointing down his jeans, cut off at the knees. He never wears sunscreen and I've never seen him burn; his skin just gets darker and more like leather every day.

He moved here seven years ago to play Junior C hockey. People say the C stands for "cut," as in, "Windsor just cut Wade Smith, so now he plays in Currie," the town as empty as outer space where a guy goes to *work on his game* or *grow into his body* before he quits hockey outright. But C's not the lowest league, D is. That *actually* stands for "development." D teams groom players for B, the steppingstone before Major Junior, the Ontario Hockey League, the O. As in "orbit." With teams in London, Windsor, Sarnia and even Michigan, junior hockey's the sun in Currie and Centennial Arena is Cape Canaveral, where teenage girls wait for the next rocket out, like I did.

Wade was the Comets' sixth defenceman, heavy-hitting and slow on his skates. I never pretended he'd make the pros, but his marks were good enough that some forgotten-about hockey team at some football-crazy college in some place like Boise, Idaho would have given him a scholarship, had he applied. Story of a lot of guys out here. Wade never got back to the O, and he didn't plan beyond Grade Twelve, so next thing you know he's settled in Currie, just working at Gable's, for now. We met at the counter always littered with catalogues—everything to hide the greener grass on your side of the fence—and a month later, we started dating, if you can call it that. We *date* and *go out* like kids in fifties movies *go steady*, but there aren't many actual dates. I was seven when the Wizard Cinema closed, and the only sit-down restaurant in town is Wang's Chinese, a dirty little room across Main Street from Brewskie's where people get take-out but no one eats in. To have a date somewhere nice you need to drive to London, which most people don't manage before they're seventeen. We were older than that when we met, but until we moved in together a date meant a video in Wade's apartment above Darla's Flowers, volume cranked to drown out the sport trucks with no mufflers as they roared up and down the main drag, Main Street, County Road 17.

Where Wade and I live now, Lyle Street, there's not even a barrier where the pavement ends, just greyed wooden posts, rusty fence wire and cornfield as far as you can see. It's a subdivision from the sixties, when Currie didn't boom; the four houses that *were* built are regularly sold, and thoroughly trashed, by a stream of twenty-something single guys who work at the Ritter plant, buying when their jobs feel safe then unloading when they get laid off anyway. We bought ours just over a year ago, peeling white paint and missing shingles and all, with a plan to fix it up then sell big to a commuter from the city, who'll go on like an idiot about small towns and *a slower pace of life*; if anything, stuff happens faster here, and it's usually because the girl's pregnant. That's not our story, thank God, but this spring Wade proposed regardless.

We drove to this fancy restaurant in London with a view of the Thames, near the century homes in Old South, and for dinner we had the specials because they're bigger and they're always a good deal. Wade wanted to stroll through the park afterward and watch the sun set over the river, but I had told Jessie, who'll be my maid-of-honour, that we'd meet everyone at Brewskie's. Of course we would. It was Friday.

In the pickup Wade sulked the whole way back to Currie. He's two years older than me, but I told him to grow up anyway when we got out at the bar. I kind of regret it now.

Inside we found Jessie at a table with Mike Carrion. His brown eyes widened and he smiled when he saw us, but when Wade shook his head Mike flagged down the waitress and ordered Jager shots, which we downed before Jessie dragged him off. He's no dancer, but at Brewskie's what counts is that you try. Most guys don't. Middle-aged women line the bar every week, believing their dream man will walk in tonight. After a few years they finally hone in on the guys down the rail who drink made-in-London Labatt beers and yell "Faggot Frog!" at the ones who buy Molson, knowing full well at least one is a Tremblay.

From the dance floor Jessie waved over Mike's shoulder. I stood up and reached for Wade's hand but he pulled it away.

"Oh, *come on*," I said. "Are you *still* mad? You're such a child sometimes."

He pulled a green velvet box from his pocket and tossed it on the table. It skipped toward me and slid to a stop near the edge.

Wade said, "You really should've come for a walk."

I picked it up and pretended the surprise wasn't blown —what else comes in boxes like this?—but I gasped when I opened it.

I said, "Wade, does this mean—"

"Yeah," he muttered.

I looked down at the ring and its three little diamonds. The biggest one leapt from the centre. It must have cost a fortune.

"Yes," I said, then "Yes! Wade, yes!" I cried. "Yes! *Yes!*"

My screams carried over the music. Everyone stopped dancing and turned to look, so for show I jumped into his arms. He wasn't ecstatic like I was, but then again, he doesn't really *do* ecstatic. Sometimes you'd think he's made of ice. But he caught me and I kissed him and I held the open box above his head. The stones caught the bar lights in red and blue and green and drew hoots and applause from the crowd.

My brother and some friends kidnapped Wade last weekend for his bachelor party in Huron Beach, where they played golf and drank beer and hit on coked-out cougars at Piranhas, the seedy bar at the bottom of the strip. I wasn't going to retaliate but Jessie insisted. She even called my boss and got me this weekend off.

Six of us eat dinner at an Italian place in London, Garofalo's, downtown on Richmond. It's a Friday in May: the restaurant's full of high schoolers laying groundwork for the prom, not drinking and taking the bus home. Our table empties four bottles of wine, but Jessie doesn't have any. She's chauffeuring us in her mom's minivan.

"Tonight's the real deal," she says, and for a moment I imagine a super-stretch limo and all of us stepping out at Fifth Avenue, which even if it's in London is a pretty ritzy club. We step onto the red carpet fifteen potato pounds lighter, bodies firm in silhouette designer dresses. Flashbulbs snap and teenaged hordes cry that they love us. And then I remember. We're going to Brewskie's. I'll be in a tacky pink veil, and though it's a girls' night Wade will be there. He says he understands if we play all the games, and he even said that he could stay home; but like the sign says, Brewskie's is The Only Bar in Town. I couldn't ask Wade to do that. He still doesn't know many people here other than Brian, who's only home on leave until the day after the wedding, and Mike, who's in from London and crashing in our parents' spare room with Paula, this new girlfriend from Western we haven't met yet.

On our way into Brewskie's Jessie hands me the list. It's in seven or eight hands and it covers all the classics.

Get a photo dancing between two hot young studs.
Come home with a pair of boxers.
Kiss a guy who's not Wade. On the lips.

If we were in Huron Beach where we don't know anyone, I'd do it all in ten minutes with two juiceheads and move on. At home I'm most afraid of the kiss, but it's one night, it's senseless, and it's more for the other girls than me — if I show Wade the list after he's had a few, he probably won't care if I plant one on Mike. It could only be Mike.

But Paula ... no one accounted for Paula.

We order drinks and head for the dance floor, where girls we haven't talked to since high school flock around us. Someone — Jessie — has tipped a couple of guys off, and already one's approaching with his shorts in his hand. They're clean, thank God, so I play it up for a few seconds, wearing them on my veil like a tiara. The girls all scream. The first ones to stop pull the lists from their purses and mechanically strike out a line.

Above the dance floor, on the riser, DJ Eric leans into his mic, turning on his Ultra Cool Voice. "Make sure to say hi to Stella Callaghan tonight," he says. He's worked here so long no one calls him just Eric, and these days he sounds like an infomercial. "This is her *stagette*. When you see her next week, she'll be Stella *Smith*!"

The girls scream again. It's too much. I grab Jessie's elbow and we make for the bathroom. When we open the door she sticks an arm in front of me. I stop and we watch someone we've never seen here before stare into the mirror under her Betty Page cut. She has an open tube of lipstick in her hand, arm frozen at a right angle, and she hasn't put any on her lips yet. Her reflection is centred in a frame drawn in black marker, probably by the same person that wrote *FOR A GOOD TIME CALL 519–URA–SLUT* above it. She looks at the ceiling and breathes, "How the hell did I get here?" Jessie and I look at each other; Jessie speaks first.

"You must be Paula," she says. "I'm Jessie."

The stranger doesn't turn her head, doesn't make eye contact even in the mirror — she just says, "I know." A faint smile lifts her lips and she brings the red tube to them.

Two drinks, ten songs, and half the list later, Wade walks in wearing his old Comets jersey, number 76. He joins Brian and Mike, who are in untucked plaid shirts and scabby jeans, at a table with Paula and a guy I don't know. His jeans fit closer, navy and expensive, and above them he wears a tailored black dress shirt. His long hair is trimmed instead of hanging out of a ball cap in a ponytail. He's definitely not from around here.

I catch myself staring as a tray arrives, ten shots and ten beers. I turn away and watch sideways as they down the liquor. Paula lags on the second. They each take two Blues.

Jessie grabs my shoulder and points to the door. The Brown twins have arrived and they're beelining toward me, convinced they still qualify as two hot young studs. Gary's still in shape after four years in the O, but he's been back since the NHL passed him over last June, working with his dad at Ritter and drinking at Brewskie's with

Jake, who quit hockey at fourteen and has the gut now to prove it. Gary's hips sandwich me into Jake's blubbery middle and it makes me glad Wade doesn't skate well. Jessie's camera flashes. The girls unfold their papers.

When the song ends I free myself and make for the bar, where I make my own double order. I take the drinks to Wade's table and pull up another chair.

"This is my friend Gianluigi," Mike says, pointing to the new guy. "He's an exchange student from a small town in Italy. He came down with us" — Mike laughs — "for a once in a lifetime experience." He shouts over the music, "Gianluigi! This is Stella!"

Wade adds, "My fiancée."

"Hi," I say.

Gianluigi looks into my eyes.

"Lucky man," he says through a heavy accent. He glances at Wade then looks back to me. "Are you having fun?"

Wade grumbles, "*Oh* yeah. She's got a whole *list* of it."

Mike looks down at the table.

Paula clutches his hand.

Wade snorts.

Brian stares through Gianluigi.

Gianluigi says, "Show me."

I hand him the paper. The kiss is all that's left and I think Wade knows it. I start to say "It's almost — " but Gianluigi stands up. He puts his hands on the back of my head and kisses me. Full on the lips. As he pulls away his bangs brush my face.

I exhale.

I open my eyes.

Mike and Brian each have one of Wade's arms and Brian's on his feet, blocking the Italian. A rap song's slow bass gives the standoff a heartbeat and again, the whole bar is watching.

Gianluigi meets Wade's glare with a lopsided smile. He shrugs.

"There," he says. "All finished. Now go get married."

Teeth crack Wade's stone face and he laughs sharply, then in rhythmic bursts, until he's gasping with tears down his cheeks. Mike and Brian release him and the crowd starts applauding, led by Jessie in a chant of *"Stel-la! Stel-la!"* as I climb on the table. I raise the list over my head and rip frantically. Pieces flutter to the floor. I reach down and grab Wade by the jersey. He stands and I kiss him, softly, then hungrily. For show I leap into his arms. He cradles me against his torso and it's still hard and muscular. No matter where he takes me, we'll end up back here, but as we burst through the door I imagine a Ferrari—bright red, roof open, and zooming down a vineyard-lined highway. In the streetlights my hair leaves a long shining tail.

Ode

BRIAN

Reading Mike's journal felt wrong, but I didn't get a choice. I found out it existed when his mother delivered the green notebook to his and Paula's rented house on the edge of Currie. I started to say, "Maybe we shouldn—", but Paula lunged in front of me and took it. Susan buried her head in Paula's shoulder before leaving and whispered, "Thanks for showing me this."

Paula led me up the stairs and we entered the second bedroom, where the desk had been cleared and Mike's mementoes piled neatly to the left: a few certificates, a framed photo of him and Paula graduating Teacher's College, and on top, a small jade carving of a bird. Paula wrapped the statuette in her fingers. She brought it to her chest. A whimper escaped her lips and she replaced it, glaring at me, having caught me staring.

"It's a nightingale," she said. "I got it for him in China."

She sat on the chair and set the book in the centre of the desk. She opened it and turned the pages sternly, determined to read them all in one sitting.

That was two days ago. Things haven't changed much. After every reading we do of Mike's eulogy, she opens the book again.

Today, she whines when she reaches the end.

"Brian, you *have* to read it."

"It's none of my business."

"You're his oldest friend!"

This is the third time I've ever met her, and already, she's yelling at me.

I keep my voice even.

"If he'd wanted me to read it, he'd have shown me."

She snaps, "You're a callous asshole, you know that?"

I sit heavily on the bed and it bounces beneath me. If I've learned anything about Paula, it's that resisting is pointless. In a minute she'll start beating her fists on the walls, turning her face blue. I reach out, she thrusts the book into my hand and I open it in the middle to a page that's Xed over. The next one is missing. I flip until I find something I *can* read, some long ramble about softball that's really about Jessie Mueller. He always went gaga over girls. I turn the page and entirely skip what's next, the stuff about Paula. I doubt she's any different, though she tells me she and Mike had been together five years; I guess I hadn't seen him in a while. I turn more pages and last, before the blank end pages, is a screed about his father. I read two emotional paragraphs and then close the book. No one should see this. But at the desk, Paula pouts above her pink sweater. Her face is kind of ruddy, and her lipstick's too red; her black dye-job screams *poser*.

We've been stopping and starting for two days now, arguing about what to tell and what to leave out. Which ones best represent Mike. She wants to use the whole notebook, and her expression is falling. She's going to start crying again. Fuck. I re-open to a part about a funeral that must've been his grandfather's — everyone remembers Tom Burford's suicide. I settle on a section about a Scout Camp we volunteered at when we were fourteen. I was there, I don't need to relive it, but I take a small pad from my jacket and scribble some notes. Paula looks on, almost smiling.

As I hand her back the book, I wonder what Mike would want. The truth is, I don't know anymore. It's been almost ten years since we left Currie Township, Mike to study English at Western and me to the army, St-Jean, Quebec. We expected to still see each other all the time: Thanksgiving, Christmas, Slack Week for him and summer leave for me. We even planned a trip to Europe after his second year, but it fell through. We'd barely talked since.

Two nights ago, Mike jumped off the River Road Bridge, just outside Currie, and he died in the Waubnakee. The coroner said he drowned after head trauma from the fall. But we jumped all the time when we were kids, in winter, even, until that first year apart, when — drunk and home for Christmas — we set out to see who had gained more weight. The bridge is so low, you can't hurt yourself even when the water's frozen. I went first and I heard the cracking sounds the moment I landed. Mike watched me from above as I high-tailed it off the ice, his hand on the railing as he knelt in the snow, laughing. Really laughing.

Killing himself.

Had he died any other way, I'd tell this one tomorrow. It's a perfect closer, too, I can hear it: "When his mother asked, 'Well if Brian asked you to jump off a bridge with him …?' my oldest friend, Mike Carrion, said 'Yes.'" I understand, though. We've got to get it right tomorrow because after death, a person only lives in words, his own and other people's. His *story*. Paula's taking it awfully literally, though, even for an English major, sitting there and leafing through the pages again and again. I'd rather we just get to the point. People are going to miss Mike, and it's sad that he died. He was a great friend, once.

I cap my pen and put it in my pocket, and then I say her name.

Paula

I HEAR HIM, I'm just ignoring him. *God.* It's like he can't see I'm in the middle of something. *Just reading my soulmate's last words, jerk-off.* But of course, Brian doesn't stop. He says my name again, drawing it out, with about seventeen *A*s and *U*s between the *P* and *L*.

And again.

"Paula!"

"*What*, Brian? What do you want?"

"We're almost finished," he says, checking his watch. "We're just under time and we've got lots to say. Let's do one more read-through."

A read-through. Like a weekday-morning seminar at some office job.

What Brian doesn't know is that you can't rehearse eulogies. You just stand up and see what comes out—even if you're left a bawling mess. Crying at a funeral's not weird; *not* crying is. You come across like the journalist with the obituary on file, three-quarters written and waiting.

Brian still expects me to answer. In his jeans and four-season jacket and balding already, he's pathetic, overcompensating with an expensive silver watch that's too big for him. The spoils of war, probably. I exaggerate a sigh from the back of my throat and hope to gas him with disgust. When it fails I say, "Sure." I don't look up.

I just want to finish this story.

> *Reid Watson threw the party he threw every summer and it fell the night before Doctor Laskey's final. As usual, Summer School was proving itself an oxymoron, but I was one credit shy and determined to graduate. Watching everyone else move on in April really drove it home, and the sublets in the dingy bungalows on Huron Street were quieter than ever, empty for the summer. I stopped by Reid's for a beer. Okay, three. The few guys who stayed in town to play on his softball team were there: Gary Connor and his girlfriend Stacey, Jumbo Joe Polack—not actually his last name, but all anyone could spell—and Craig and Michelle, and Jeff and—*

Of course it's true. When he really started writing, everything was and he left nothing out. The list goes on for a while. Things get better when I show up.

She was a year younger than me. Maybe more like two and a half. It doesn't matter because I didn't find out. Having failed last summer session because of just this party, I knew I was doomed to leave early, but still I stared, watching her strum Reid's guitar on the porch and pretend she was shy, singing softly, holding it back. The next morning I wrote an exam worth a bright shining seventy-one, and afterward, instead of telling Doctor Laskey to stuff it, that I'd failed Romantic Lit for the last time, I just bolted to Reid's to ask about The Nightingale.

Seriously. Like in Keats, or The Emperor And The. He only called me that once to my face, and I laughed at him. "What a cheeseball," I said. "I will never date you." In China two years later, I bought him the figurine; a peace offering for a long-forgotten slight.

"Fifteen seconds," Brian says, checking the damned watch. He turns his wrist to show me. "I'm starting when the second hand gets to the twelve."

"I can tell time, Brian."

He breathes in. Checks again. Goes.

"Your friend and mine, Michael Carrion, will be sorely missed," he begins. "Mike's girlfriend Paula and I are honoured to be asked to memorialize a man who—"

I quit listening and let my eyes glaze over. *Memorialize?* Is that even a word? It's so unfeeling. He reads into the mirror with his hands at his sides, making sure to keep them out of his pockets. I don't refocus until I hear "Scout Camp."

"We're at this cattle ranch, not far out of town," he's saying. "It's an overnight hike, in the fall, and kids from every troop in MacKinnon County are running around playing war, shooting each other with the sticks they've gathered for firewood.

"But Mike, he wants no part of this. He picks up our tent, which is still limp on the ground, and tells me to take the other side. We carry it into the middle of this flat and set it up. A private camp, for just the two helpers from First Currie troop. That night, once the kids are all in bed, we make a small fire and cook canned soup, and we spend the night talking about every girl in Grade Nine, all spaghetti straps and nice legs and whose chest is still flat." He laughs to set up his mandatory levity: "Which didn't do so much for me, of course."

I've read this one. It doesn't go anywhere after the body parts. Playing it for a laugh at himself is really Brian's only hope. The better stuff's all in my part: undergrad, Teacher's College, English classes in China, Mike's first job, moving home with a Toronto Girl.

"When we wake up we're surrounded by a hundred head of longhorn," Brian says. "We didn't know it, but we pitched our tent in their pasture, and now, all these cows are lowing and grazing and stomping around us, and the two of us are just waiting, cowering in our sleeping bags, hoping they take off soon."

They do. The end.

A better story would have Mike reassure Brian, or crack a joke, or maybe even get up and chase away the longhorns, but that must not be how it happened. No matter. The mourners will laugh anyway. Easy pickings at a funeral. Brian chose a story and delivered it unflinchingly: off-book, with no tears, and no choking up. Ten out of ten.

"That's just one of our great memories," he says.

I forgot about the slam-bang conclusion, for bonus marks.

"And though we might not have seen each other much these last few years, I know in my heart that Mike cherished our childhood just like I—"

"Brian, stop."

He looks at his watch, to mark time.

"What?"

"When did you last see him?"

He takes his speech from the desk and raps it on the wood, like a news anchor wrapping up.

"I've known him since Grade Nine."

"That's not what I asked—when?"

The hand holding his papers drifts to his side.

"I guess it was ... four years ago. Before Afghanistan."

"You haven't seen him since you've been home."

His eyes bugged in protest.

"I've been in Wainwright. Do you even know where that is?"

I don't, but I won't let him change the subject.

"Do *you* even know what happened the night he died?"

"He was walking home."

"From ...?"

"From Brewskie's."

I shake my head.

"No. He had just left our place."

Brian's eyes widen.

"So how'd he wind up dead in the river?"

I imagine punching his accusing face. Is he saying it was *my* fault?

"He had just gotten some bad news. He went out to clear his head."

"What was it?"

"His dad."

"Something happened to John?"

"Not John," I say. "Ray. Who knows how he found our number, but he called up out of nowhere. I guess he married someone else, a year after he left Susan, and had three other kids. He asked Mike if they could reconnect — just like that, a whole second family. Like nothing had happened."

Brian sits down on the bed. He runs a hand over what's left of his hair.

"First call since …?"

"Since ever."

"And that's why he killed himself."

"You're such an idiot, Brian. He didn't kill himself."

"So what, it was an accident? He *fell* off the bridge?"

"I don't know," I say. "I *do* think he jumped—"

"But?"

"But I don't think he wanted to die."

Brian looks down at his black boots.

I thought Susan had told him all this.

"Mike talked a lot that night about old memories," I say. "About China, and how he'd moved beyond this place. He mentioned so many people I'd never heard of, kids who had moved away when he was still in elementary school only to resurface one day in Grade Ten in the smoking pit at CHS, who no one asked but everyone knew lived with an aunt or a grandparent now, or worse, one, or *both* of the parents they'd left town with—". I catch my breath. "He couldn't believe he'd wound up back here, anyway, and he said he was sorry for dragging me down with him—that he'd understand if I went back to Toronto."

"So what did you say?"

Suspicious. Still blaming me.

"I said that whatever happened, we'd do it together. His contract was just a year—so what if it was at his old high school?—and I was getting calls for sub work in London. It was experience, and before long we'd take it somewhere else: Toronto, or Hamilton if we had to, or even England or somewhere. There was no rush."

Brian raises a hand to his mouth. He nibbles a thumbnail.

"So he was okay? Last time you saw him?"

I exhale.

"He was really upset that everyone he had known was either a burnout or long gone, hung over every day on the line at Ritter or never to be heard from again. He said, '*Oldest friend* and *best friend* aren't synonyms.'"

Brian shifts on the bed. I pin him with my eyes.

"Yes. He mentioned your name."

"I'm sure he did," Brian says. "I saw him that night, too."

"*What?*"

BRIAN

I SHOULDN'T HAVE told her. Really. It's the last thing she needs. And now, if we don't get past it, we'll never get this speech done.

"I was on course at Wolseley," I say. "I came to visit my parents. We ordered Chinese, and afterward I went out to Brewskie's with Wade and Stella ... do you know my sister?"

Paula stamps her foot. I'd better cut to the chase.

"I don't know when he got to the bar, but Mike was stinking drunk when I saw him. Did he have anything at home?"

"Two beers."

"I didn't notice him until he got loud, when Willy cut him off. I guess he'd been there a while ..."

"So you ...?"

"So I went over and talked him down. I told him I'd walk him home."

Paula's lips quiver.

"You *walked home with him*?"

It spreads to her whole face.

"Why didn't he *get* home?"

I feel the sweat gathering, moist beneath my watch. I unclasp it and set it on the bed.

"We had an argument."

She grits her teeth.

"I was trying to help."

"Big mistake when he gets talking about Ray," she says, scoffing. "God, Brian. What did you say?"

"I said, 'Maybe seeing him will help everyone move on.'"

"That wouldn't have made it better."

"No." I don't mean to laugh. "You're right."

Paula scowls.

"He said I was missing the point — that I was just another army asshole like Ray and that it must be nice to always have it all figured out. He was really angry. He didn't understand why Ray would abandon them but man up for someone else."

"And then?"

"And then he got quiet for a minute. We just looked at each other. He said, 'I don't get it. You and I both got out of here, but I messed it up. You'll drive to London tomorrow and get on a plane back to wherever the hell you live now, and once you're gone, this place will swallow me whole.'"

Paula sinks in the chair.

"Anything else?"

"He took a swing at me."

"Did you hit him back?"

"He was so drunk." I smile. "It wasn't much of a punch."

She doesn't find it funny.

"I just said, 'Fine, Mike. Get yourself home,' and turned around. I left him on Main Street. I guess he carried on … past your house and out of town … and when he got to the—"

Paula's face goes white.

"No." She shakes her head. "You must have said something else. Come on. What did you say?"

Fuck. Well. I've come this far.

"I told him that I wished I hadn't run into him. After he tried to hit me. And that maybe we'd be better off just remembering how things were when we were kids." I put my head in my hands. That's all I want to say, but I feel her hot glare. It draws the rest out of me. "He said, 'Maybe you're right.' And for what it's worth, he was pretty calm."

She squints, perplexed.

"I asked if he was all right to get back," I say, but the next part clangs in my brain. "He said, 'Sure thing.' And then he said ... 'Goodbye.'"

I feel my jaw relax, and the first tears run onto my cheeks. I don't look at her. I just croak, "I'm so sorry."

Paula

Well, what do you know? I thought. *Brian is human.*

When he started to cry I sat down on the bed, and immediately, he keeled over. His head landed in my lap.

"Oh my God. Oh, God. It's my fault," he moaned, tears on my jeans and his chest heaving. "I killed him!"

I took him by the shoulders.

"No, you didn't."

He sniffed. "Mike jumped because even his oldest friend walked out on him."

Melodramatic, and wrong.

"Brian, you said you just wanted to remember being kids. Right?"

He sat up and put his hands to his eyes, correcting the aberration, this sudden show of emotion. He stretched his cheeks as he wiped them. He nodded.

"I think he decided to be a kid again," I said.

Brian dried his nose on his khaki sleeve.

"It was a mistake," I said. "It wasn't suicide."

Brian clenched his fists.

"What's it matter?" he snarled. "Everyone's decided already."

"Not everyone."

I took the notebook from the desk and flipped to the very back, where a newer pen had marked the yellow pages.

"*I remember summer afternoons with Brian,*" I read aloud. "*We're not friends anymore, which I feel bad about, but—*"

I looked at Brian. He held his breath.

"*—now, with everything that's happened, that's all I want to keep. The rest of it has faded, been thrown under a blanket. I can't make sense of it. Most of it, I can't even remember. All I have now are those days, laying our towels on the banks, daring each other and jumping.*"

Brian reached for the notebook.

"Let me see that," he said.

I pulled back and shielded it with my body.

"I can't believe—"

"Run with what you have."

"You think that's best?" he asked.

I nodded.

"You're talking about the good parts, when you were in high school, and you never suggest that he killed himself."

Brian stared off.

"I should have read the whole thing."

"You already had your mind made up."

He inhaled and gathered himself, looking first out the window.

"I'm sorry," he said.

And then, ever the taskmaster, he stood up. He looked at the watch on the bed.

"Okay," he said. "Your turn. What will you say tomorrow?"

I took my speech from the desk — three pages, typed the night before.

"I know that he didn't want to die," I said. "This is just a terrible twist of fate." A useful cliché, and now, the big finish, like the public speaking people teach: "He had always written, but he was starting to work at it — going back to his old journals and editing them, making something someone else could read. It was magical: he was excited, for once.

"Awakening. That's how I'll remember Mike."

I looked up from my papers. I hadn't cried at all.

"It's good," Brian said.

We knew what to expect before we finished writing. People had lined up out the funeral home door for visitation, so Susan moved the service to the Currie High School gym. In the folding chairs now are Mike's extended family members and the other teachers with their students. In the back are a lot of those small-town types, who met Mike maybe once, maybe when he was ten, but who still can't imagine not being here.

"He was only twenty-nine," they whisper. "Such a shame."

I sit onstage behind the open curtain, between an

industrial-sized trash can and Brian's empty chair, watching him sing his mechanical song. He says his speech word for word and never looks down — even better than he did in the mirror yesterday. I notice Jessie Mueller in the back row in her skating jacket, eyes locked on Brian the whole time. When he steps away from the podium, each silent second tamps the crowd, and when he's finally out of sight he exhales. It betrays the weight it carries.

The minister takes Brian's place. He leans over the microphone. "And now, I'd like to call on Michael's girlfriend, Paula Wells." Jessie hurriedly sidesteps out of her row toward the exit. I stand and inhale. Brian flashes a miniature thumbs up. It's corny but he means it. I edge between him and a cage of red dodge-balls, but then I turn back to the trash can. I drop my speech in. From my skirt pocket, I pull out a page I ripped from the green notebook.

"Paula, no," Brian whispers. "You don't know what he wanted to leave out."

On stage I rest the paper under the lamp in front of me. I look at the title, *The Jade Nightingale*, and the beginning, which he had shown to only me. I take a deep breath and I form the words, but when I open my mouth all that comes out is a sob. I drop my head into my arms on the wood.

Brian taps his watch backstage.

Nine more minutes.

My throaty gasp echoes through the speakers. It rattles the walls.

Nobody Looks That Young Here

*T*AXIS CART THE fresh faces toward the university, and the people left behind are the ones from around here, obstacles on the way to the exit: a maintenance guy in pale brown holding an extra large Tim's cup; a ticket collector gathering her jacket; an older pot-bellied man in plaid looking at the ceiling, expressionless while his wife clutches their teenage son to her cat sweater.

The boy was me, twenty-eight years ago, saying, "I'll be fine, it's not even far," then striding to the platform without looking back. I'm nearly fifty now, but in London I still sit on the hard blue seats and wait for a ride from my parents. The mid-morning train carries either students or my kind: adopted Torontonians home for an afternoon funeral. I've missed quite a few since I left Currie Township, but this time I can't stay away.

I READ ABOUT Mike Carrion online, in the *London Free Press* obits. Nobody calls me when people die anymore. His surviving aunt, Claire, was with my brother, Scott, when we were teenagers, and I remember Susan, too, leaving school when the kid was born; she came back briefly the next year before she gave up entirely. I had never seen him before his photo was in the paper: farmer tan, burnt nose, sandy hair messed from swimming, on a Thai beach with a pretty brunette, *Mike* ♥ *Paula* toe-etched in the sand. Paula's grin shone compared to Mike's featherweight grimace, a smile that reminded me of my own at that age.

ON THE TRAIN, when I tried to predict Susan's state, I settled on some mix of catatonic and numb. I didn't even consider drunk. Before the ceremony she spots me on the fringe of the Currie High School gym. Under her greying straw hair her age-puckered mouth forms an *O*. Behind her glasses the crinkles multiply. She hurries toward me.

"What are you—," she says, "it's great to see you, Dave," and she wraps me in a vodka-scented hug, closer than it should be. It's as though she presumed *me* dead. I shouldn't have come. I'm upstaging the kid.

When she finally lets go, she says, "I can't believe you came all the way from Toronto."

"It's not that f—"

She hugs me again.

"Thank you," she says.

I WEDGE INTO the back row with the farm boy second cousins: a grey-suited kicker among a black-clad offensive line. From the stage Paula eulogizes, or tries to, breaking down and rushing off, which sends a wave of hushed chatter through the crowd. I'm sure most people have come just to hear what Susan will say, but she doesn't leave the front row where she sniffles softly. A bare arm strokes her back from a sleeveless black dress next to her. I'm not listening to the minister when he reclaims the podium; the arm is lightly muscled, the dress sleek. The brown hair almost to the waist is without a hint of silver. Nobody looks that young here.

But is Claire back for the funeral, or *back* back?

Of course she stays facing forward, neck rod-straight, and she follows along with the hymn and Psalm 23, keeping hold of her sister through the service's final words, a reminder about coffee and sandwiches at Currie Presbyterian after interment. The pamphlets say *internment*. And Mike was an English teacher. His former colleagues rise first and shepherd students back to class, leaving a small contingent for the trip to River Road Cemetery, which is closer than ever this spring to washing into the Waubnakee with the melting snow.

I scan the gym for someone I can ask for a ride. I recognize a few faces, but I'd have to make them recognize me, Bill and Gloria's not-so-prodigal son who left town after that awful accident. The idiot who tried to re-open the movie theatre. I linger just long enough to get a view of the family. Susan sags into the black dress and I finally see Claire's smooth face. It closes its eyes and moves its lips, whispering. The eyes meet mine when they reopen. The manicured brows rise. The mouth forms a faint smile, then *Dave*, and the left hand sweeps subtly toward the double doors—a sort of *See you at the cemetery* that I answer with a small nod. I disappear into the herd between gym and cafeteria and exit to the student parking lot, a path to Main Street I thought I'd never take again. The storefronts are boarded up like they were when I left town.

I sit on a brand-new bench when I reach the old train station, the object of the Save Our Heritage plaque in front of it. The black roof and grey trusses and dulling white trim have been painted pale brown, and dark green, and cream. Young shrubs have been planted out front. Still, no train has stopped here in twenty years. I watch the hearse and cars behind it head out Main Street toward the township, then I wait a while before I start a slow walk to the church.

IT'S THIRTY-ONE YEARS since my last visit to Currie Presbyterian—more if you don't count Christmas Eves—but the platters are served by the same church ladies, in their eighties now but going strong, until, until, until. As always, tables are in three long rows—it wouldn't matter whether it was a wedding, the Harvest Supper or a wake—and the sandwiches are still made with Price-Mart white bread and canned tuna or egg salad from a tub. The coffee is dishwatery as ever. The floor made of musty wooden slats seems more worn than I remember, but it might just be the contrast with the renovated back wall, where a new white vestibule and wide door lead to a just-built ramp. Mike's family walks up it, led by swaying Susan, who Paula supports with a forearm. A younger woman follows who must be Mike's sister, Nancy, then Claire. The black dress is finally a little rumpled.

"Dave," she says. "Nice of you to come."

I look down.

"Well, it's not about me."

"Or me," she says, tilting her head toward Susan. She exhales and a silence sets in. "Still in Toronto?" she finally asks.

I've never been much for small talk, but sometimes ...

"Yeah. You?"

She shakes her head.

"I moved back when Mom was dying." Little smile. "Five years ago, I guess."

"I'd never have thought—"

"I know, right?" She stifles a laugh—this is a funeral, after all. "Me, who tore out of here, never to be seen again ..."

"That's two of us," I say.

"So what do you do now?"

I look past her.

"I've been at TD Bank since I was twenty-five," I say. "I've done pretty much everything you can do there, but I'll never get promoted any higher, because—"

Stop. It's boring.

"What about you?" I ask.

"Teacher," she says. "Elementary. Off today, obviously."

"Married?"

"I was. He wouldn't move with me." She looks away for a second. "You?"

"No," I say, "never." And to avoid saying more about it, I ask, "Any kids?"

"Two boys."

I glance around the room.

"Did they come?"

She looks away from me.

"They've never really known their cousins."
"Still ..."
"Still."

Over Claire's shoulder, I see Susan lean into Nancy, burying her head in the dirty blond hair on the thick shoulder.

I ask, "How's she holding up?" even though I know the answer.

"Not well. She's been drinking a lot."

"And his father ...?"

She shakes her head again.

"No one's seen Ray since the 80s. He phoned Mike, though."

I don't know what to say.

"The night of the accident," she adds. "I probably shouldn't talk about it."

I nod and try to think of something.

She blurts: "Everyone's blaming Ray."

Silence again.

"How's Scott?" she asks.

"Still in Calgary ..." I say, stalling a second. "He used to tell me I should look you up, when you were still in Toronto." Here goes. "I'm sorry I never did."

"I'm sorry, too," she says. She looks away and so do I. Already the lunchers are starting to disperse; a sandwich and coffee and then back to the field, or in a lot of cases Ritter, where the afternoon shift will start soon. Dishes clatter and we turn to the sound. Susan is falling and taking a white tablecloth with her, scattering date squares and vegetables with ranch dip on the floor.

"Oh, God," Claire says, and rushes off to her sister.

THE OLD BROWN Buick is all that's left of Susan's life in the bungalow on the acre beside the tracks—the house John, then Mike, then Nancy left before Susan sold, when Vaughan's Bakery went out of business. She moved back into the empty farmhouse where she was raised, and the car's become a second home since then, forever driving to her new job at the Westmount Mall Zellers in London or all over MacKinnon County, volunteering with the church caterers.

All this I learn behind the Buick's wheel, with Susan passed out between Paula and Nancy on the backseat. Claire rides up front with me. As it turns out, I'm the only one other than Susan with a licence. Claire waved me over as my parents waited for me outside the church, her other hand on the Buick's blistered hood. She blushed when she admitted she let her licence expire in Toronto. Paula, having grown up there, had never bothered getting one; Mike used to drive her everywhere. Nancy took the train back and forth to college in Sarnia. Claire handed me the keys, brushing my hand with her soft one. After I explained through the window of Dad's Cadillac, he and Mom followed us out of town.

I've renewed every five years, but this is my first time driving since I moved away. I keep the radio off and roll too slowly onto Main Street, swivelling my head at the intersection for cars and pedestrians that aren't there. As we pass the town limit, Nancy mentions that she and Paula are staying with Susan. "To answer the phone and help with cooking and stuff." Paula adds, "And keep watch on her drinking," which sucks the air out of the car. I turn the radio on after all.

I let out a heavy breath when I park in the farmhouse laneway. Nancy and Paula get out and, each draping one of Susan's arms over their shoulders, they lead her up the porch stairs and call, "Thanks, Dave." Claire looks at me and says, "Really. Thanks," getting out of the Buick and walking to Dad's car. She pulls open the Caddy's back door and slides over to let me in. She seems to know her dress has climbed clear of her knee, but she doesn't show any intent to fix it.

WE DON'T TALK in the backseat, awkward as thirteen-year-olds on a movie date, praying the adults won't ask.

Mom turns slightly.

"How was it?"

"What?"

"Driving."

I shrug.

"Fine."

"Do you think that maybe you'll get a car, and—?"

"Mom, really ..."

"Sorry, Dave. Sorry. It's just, it's been so long since—"

"Since," I say. "I know." I exhale. "Just because I *can* still drive doesn't mean I like to. And all the traffic, the 401 speedway? Forget it."

"But out here?" Mom says.

"Out here's the same as always," I say. "There have never been other cars on the road."

Mom purses her lips and resumes quietly facing the windshield.

"So just to your house, Claire?" Dad asks when we're nearly back to Currie.

"Actually, if it's all right," she says, looking at me, "I'd like to come and wait for the train with you."

Dad glances at me in the rear view. I return an *I-don't-know* brow lift.

"Sure thing," Dad says. We stay on Main Street until it becomes County Road 17 again and we follow it to the on-ramp, eastbound to London.

MOM AND DAD must see it coming, too. They say goodbye early and let us out at the station, making an excuse: they've been meaning to browse Home Depot's wainscoting on their next trip to the city. They say they'll come back for Claire.

In the lounge, she eyes the Tim's kiosk and says, "Coffee?"

"Sure."

"Milk or sugar?"

I shake my head. My watch shows ten to seven. Departure is at oh-five but there's no hurry—no train yet, no crush of students on a Wednesday. I pick a cold seat in the blue plastic row and in a moment Claire returns, paper cup in each hand. She gives me mine and sits beside me. I thank her and sip, burning my mouth a bit.

"So," she says. "Twelve minutes and you're out of my life again."

"Was I ever really in it?" I ask.

Her features sharpen into a hurt look.

"I was almost your family."

"Your father would have loved that."

"My father wouldn't have loved anything," she says.

We both laugh. She sighs and says, "Even if I had picked the right brother."

I blow on my coffee and sip again. She pushes a long strand of hair off her shoulder, down her back.

"What's happened all these years?" she asks.

I listen for the train but hear nothing.

"What do you mean?"

"Ten minutes," she says, smiling. "What have you done with your life?"

"I've taken some trips," I say. "Seen some great movies. I've known the odd woman."

"That's what I'm talking about. The good stuff." She smiles wider. Her teeth are still bright white and perfect.

"I've never seen much as good or bad," I say. "It's just been what it's been."

A snarky whish comes out her nose.

"The more things change," she mutters, "the more Dave McLaren stays the same."

Finally a whistle sounds in the distance. A soft rumble nears.

"And what will you do now?" she asks, putting a hand on my forearm.

I say, "I'll probably go to work tomorrow."

She furrows her brow.

"Goddammit," she says. "I'm coming onto you, Dave."

"I know."

"And you …"

"And I can't," I say, making to get up.

She squeezes. One fingernail scratches me.

"My kids are gone," she says. "My parents are dead.

My sister's my only friend and she's never been anywhere." Her eyes start to plead as she stands. "I've still got some money from the Toronto house—the divorce. We could be happy."

"You could," I say.

She frowns.

"But I'm not."

"So why are you here?" I ask.

"It's just—it's who we are."

I shake my head and pull my arm away.

"No it isn't," I say, standing up. "Not us."

She scowls and says, "Fine. Go." And then she stands and shouts, "Fuck you!" as the train whistle drowns her out. When it finishes she's still standing there.

I say, "You're just like I remember—just like in high school."

"Is that supposed to make me feel better?" she snaps.

I step back and look closely at her face. Her jaw is soft and her eyes are tender; perfect makeup, not a crease in sight. Her mouth hangs slightly open as I put my arms around her. I kiss her gently on the cheek. Brakes squeal. "Take care of your sister," I say. "And look me up if you come back." But with finality she shoves me off. I turn and walk toward the glass door. It slides opens automatically and I step onto the platform. A sob creeps through the pane and Claire's teacher heels click, slowly then faster as they fade. I don't turn around. On the train, I sink into a window seat and let my lungs fall into time with the chugging engine. As the train leaves the city, dusk turns to night, and outside cars barns houses blur, back into dark and nothingness.

Afterword

With the exception of "Young Buck", written in early 2016, the stories in this book were initially composed between 2009 and 2012. "Funeral" and "The Expiry Dates" were born of my first-ever writing course, Richard Scarsbrook's Expressive Writing I at George Brown College. Thank you, Richard, for taking me seriously.

"The Expiry Dates" was the first of my stories to be published, in *Broken Pencil*'s 2011 Death Match contest, a savage, week-long online affair involving hourly voting and an open, heavily-trolled comment board—seven white-knuckled, unsleeping, friend-harassing days for which I'm immensely grateful, as they galvanized me as a writer and somehow avoided scaring me off the whole enterprise or my friends and family off of their continued support.

For publishing the stories in this collection in slightly or very different versions, thank you also to the editors of *The Broken City*, *White Wall Review*, *Nōd*, *The Sunday Paper* (Wooden Rocket Press) *The Dalhousie Review*, *echolocation*, *The Prairie Journal of Canadian Literature*, *Sterling*, *Exile Literary Quarterly* and *Carter V. Cooper Short Fiction*

Anthology, In/Words, Maple Tree Literary Supplement, The Acrobat (Tightrope Books), *The Loose Canon* (Siren Song Publishing), *Scrivener Creative Review* and *Great Lakes Review*.

"Mercy" was a finalist for the Carter V. Cooper Short Fiction Prize in 2012. It also earned a Summer Literary Seminars Unified Literary Contest fellowship that year, as "The Expiry Dates" had in 2010. Thank you SLS for the opportunity to participate in the 2011 workshop in Vilnius, Lithuania.

"Five Stages of Sorry" benefited greatly from advice and encouragement provided by Farzana Doctor, when she was Writer-in-Residence at the Toronto Public Library and my manuscript had the good fortune to be plucked from the pile. In a small writing group Farzana put together, Nicole Baute and Sarah Simon provided helpful feedback on some of these stories. Sarah read the entire manuscript, too, in 2013, as did Julie McArthur, which was a remarkable achievement given how far the book's come since then. Many of the stories in this book were also improved in the F&G Writers Workshop that Julie co-ordinates; thanks also to members Susan Alexander, Robert Shaw, Nadia Ragbar and Brad Weber for your continued support and friendship.

The fledgling drafts of these stories, back in 2010 or so, were also read by a great many friends; thank you Marshall Bellamy, Eric Johanssen, Marcin Mokrzewski, Magda Kus, Jean Larivière, Sidonie Wybourn and others I might have forgotten for reading my work before anyone read my work.

Some lines in "The Territory" are borrowed from Emily Dickinson's "There Is No Frigate Like a Book" and Mark Twain's *Adventures of Huckleberry Finn*. François Truffaut's remark used as this book's epigraph was originally made in the French magazine *Arts* in 1959, though my source for it was the special exhibit in his honour at the Cinémathèque Française in late 2014.

Pauline Durand took me to that exhibit, and all that's happened since is still just the beginning. All my love, my favourite reader, my wife, *mon petit chat*.

About the Author

Daniel Perry's first short fiction collection, *Hamburger*, was published in 2016, and his short stories have appeared in more than 30 publications in Canada, the U.S., the U.K. and the Czech Republic. He grew up in small-town Southwestern Ontario, has an MA in Comparative Literature, and has lived in Toronto since 2006.

Printed in February 2018
by Gauvin Press,
Gatineau, Québec